NURSE'S MASQUERADE

Brent Butler was so persuasive that lovely Nurse Cara Merrill reluctantly agreed to accompany him to the fabulous Butler estate and pretend to be his debutante fiancée. Cara's real purpose, Brent told her, was to watch over his elderly uncle whose health had been mysteriously failing. Brent was suspicious of his handsome cousin, Paul, and when both men declared their love for her, Cara had to make the most important decision of her life!

JEAN CAREW

NURSE'S MASQUERADE

Complete and Unabridged

LINFORD
Leicester

First published in the
United States of America

First Linford Edition
published March 1994

British Library CIP Data

Carew, Jean
Nurse's masquerade.—Large print ed.—
Linford romance library
I. Title II.Series
813.54 [F]

ISBN 0–7089–7518–6

Published by
F. A. Thorpe (Publishing) Ltd.
Anstey, Leicestershire

Set by Words & Graphics Ltd.
Anstey, Leicestershire
Printed and bound in Great Britain by
T. J. Press (Padstow) Ltd., Padstow, Cornwall

This book is printed on acid-free paper

1

IT had been a strange interview.

Ten days afterward, Cara Merrill climbed the stairs to her small, inconvenient apartment in New York's Greenwich Village and stood at the window looking upon the uninspiring view of the red brick house next door, the water towers and crumbling chimneys of other low-roofed tenements. There was nothing about the apartment to recommend it on an unseasonably hot day in May except one thing; it was cheap.

Cara watched as a heavy-set woman emerged onto a roof three houses away and started to hang up wash. There were probably other jobs a registered nurse could get apart from hospital routine; no need to get panicky even in the face of a rapidly dwindling bank account. If she didn't like hospital routine and for some reason or other she had found herself turning against it a month ago, there was always some private duty job she might apply for.

She was a good nurse. Cara Merrill had been graduated third highest in her class. She had an inborn interest in care of the sick which had brought compliments from many of the doctors with whom she had worked. But ten days ago, after she had quit the hospital, she had wanted to do something different. She had thought of getting a post as nurse on a cruise ship. Or, since summer was coming on, she might get in touch with some dude ranch or other playground of the wealthy which might offer a job and a free vacation.

Cara Merrill had made her plans. First, by careful economy, she managed to put aside a few hundred dollars so she could stop working and take time to look around for a new post to suit her adventurous mood. Then she did all the things she had wanted to do for a long time: she slept late in the morning; went window shopping along Fifth Avenue; rented a car and drove through the countryside to see the apple blossoms and the fresh green of the spring grass. But it hadn't been much fun after all — and it was surprisingly expensive. Then she saw the ad in a Sunday newspaper:

> 'NURSE WANTED — must be experienced, blonde, willing to live in the country (large estate) June-July only. Top Salary.'

Cara Merrill wrote a rather flippant note to the box number in the paper. She did not care whether she got the job or not — or even know if she wanted it. But there had been an answer, and she had been interviewed — by a Brent Butler — in the lobby of a plush New York hotel.

She had had to make up her mind by herself. Once again she knew the isolated feeling of being an orphan.

She had never been able to confide in the few friends she had made. Her friends had always been scarcely more than acquaintances; Cara Merrill had avoided becoming involved with anyone, even those in her chosen profession. Romance? Time enough for that later, she felt. But often, in the last few days, she would have been glad of someone with whom she could talk over the job she had been offered. For it had been a very strange interview.

The man who came toward her across the shining expanse of tiled floor looked taller than he was — and he *was tall* — because he was so very thin. He was not a handsome man; not even really good-looking, Cara decided. But she liked the way he handled himself; he moved like an athlete, with an athlete's easy grace.

"You are Miss Cara Merrill?" His smile was warm and interested. And there was no doubt he approved her yellow wool suit and the big hat which she had pulled off as she came into the lobby.

"Yes, I wrote you. I'm a registered nurse. The position sounds attractive, although your description was vague. If I may say so, Mr. Butler, when people advertise for a nurse it is customary to mention who the patient is, the type of care that will be required, that sort of thing."

Butler folded his long frame into the modern chair beside hers and nodded gravely. Cara studied his face. His nose was large — well, it fitted his face. He was deeply tanned, as if he had spent some time recently in the tropics. His eyes? Gray? Blue? Hard to tell — he had a trick of narrowing them, she noticed, as if he were concentrating on a difficult problem. Did the question of hiring her present such a problem? She smiled at the thought.

"You're lovely when you smile," Brent Butler said unexpectedly. But he made it a statement of fact, not a compliment. "Let me tell you about the job, and you'll see why I couldn't put the details in an ad."

It was his uncle, Joshua Butler, who was the patient, Cara learned. He had been crippled by polio years before and was confined to a wheel chair. There was a man attendant, Fred Bates, who took care of him, had been taking care of him a long time. Uncle Josh lived on an inherited family estate on Long Island and had been in excellent health except for his infirmity. But, for no apparent reason, he had had several bouts of illness recently which had the household worried.

"What does the doctor say is the trouble?" Cara asked.

"Uncle Josh won't have a doctor near him. He says it's just something he ate, something which disagreed with him. So far he has recovered from each attack within twenty-four hours. But I am worried. I wonder if someone isn't making a deliberate attempt to poison Uncle Josh! He talks of changing his will, and there's just a possibility . . . but it's all rather complicated to explain."

"Why don't you hire a detective?" Cara asked.

"It would create a furore, and there's nothing definite to go on," Brent Butler said. "Anyhow, I thought a nurse might have some idea what causes these upsets, if she were living right on the premises and could watch Uncle Josh. Then, if necessary, I could take action and see that Uncle Josh was protected."

"But if he won't consult a doctor, surely he would object to a nurse?"

For the first time the sophisticated man who was interviewing her looked uncomfortable.

"You wouldn't come to Soundings as a nurse," he explained. "You'd come as a house guest . . . stay about two months. No one else would know you're a nurse, and you'd report to me in private whatever you found out."

"You want me to be a spy!" Cara exclaimed.

"No, not really. But you see I am very fond of Uncle Joshua. I want to know what is going on. If you should discover my suspicions are wrong — that nobody is trying to harm him but he has some serious malady — then I will insist that he have proper medical attention."

"It still sounds as if you want me to do some spying for you," Cara said stubbornly. "You'll have to give me time to think it over."

Again Brent Butler smiled. "While you're thinking it over," he said casually, "I'd like you to take into consideration the salary. I'll pay fifteen hundred dollars for the eight week period."

Cara Merrill blinked. It was a tempting amount — and it was to be paid for no work, no nursing whatever! Then a sudden thought struck her, and she asked:

"What reason are you going to give for inviting me to your uncle's home? Am I just a friend you met casually or the sister of an old college chum or what?"

"I could hardly have met you casually where I've been for the last year. I'm a construction engineer, and I've been working on a new dam in the wilds of Brazil. I didn't meet any beautiful young women there; I was rather busy." Butler looked embarrassed and did not go on for a moment.

"Well then," said Cara impatiently, "how are you going to account for me? Did you meet me at a country club dance or somewhere like that? Even so, it seems to me this sudden invitation to spend practically the whole summer at your uncle's house will have you doing some fancy explaining."

"I've thought it all out. I'll say you are my fiancée. We've just become engaged. You're the debutante daughter of a member of the firm I work for. Naturally I want you to meet my Uncle Josh."

"Meet seems hardly the word for it, if I'm to be Uncle Josh's guest for two months," Cara commented.

"Don't look for flaws in the plan," said Brent Butler. "If you want the job — and I hope you'll take it — there's no problem to having you visit Soundings as an honored guest. You can take my word for it."

No problem! Cara Merrill could see many problems involved in posing as the fiancée of a man she had just met and in living as a masquerader in the home of a man who had been embittered against all doctors, and presumably nurses, by a tragic illness the medical profession of an earlier day had been unable to conquer.

* * *

The pale beige convertible handled like a dream, Cara reflected as she drove over the Queensboro Bridge and pointed its sleek hood toward a place called Soundings on the North Shore of Long Island. It was the first day of June; also, technically, she was working.

Cara Merrill, registered nurse, smiled wryly at Cara Merrill, debutante and fiancée of Brent Butler.

The idea of changing her identity had been startling at first, but once she had decided to take the job she found the plan more or less intriguing. There had been other aspects of it which developed gradually. Perhaps, Cara thought more than once, she might have declined the job if she had realized how much change it entailed.

It had not occurred to her, for example, that her 'fiancé' — she must remember to think of him as Brent! — would insist she arrive at Soundings in a new convertible. He had told her so at the second interview. Then he whisked her off to the automobile showroom and picked out the car himself.

"I like the color," he explained; "it exactly matches your hair. And I think the gray upholstery is nice, don't you? You can have it changed if you prefer."

"By all means keep it gray," Cara murmured. "If we're going to match the color of my hair, we might as well match the color of my eyes, too. By the way, I can't accept a car as expensive as this as a present. Suppose I want to quit the job — or suppose your uncle takes a dislike to me!"

Brent Butler looked at her, his eyes narrowing in a characteristic way.

"Cara — Carita," he said in a mocking tone, "where did you get the idea I was giving you this convertible? I simply want you to make a good impression on all my family as well as my uncle. In other words, I'm *loaning* the car to you for the duration of the masquerade."

There had been another loan, also for the 'duration'. It was an old-fashioned sapphire ring surrounded by rose diamonds which sparkled now on the third finger of her left hand. Cara had loved the ring from the minute she saw it. Brent had presented it one night at dinner and had explained, when she exclaimed how lovely it was, it had belonged to his grandmother.

"I didn't realize when I started this business of getting you to pose as my fiancée," Brent said, "how it would be when I knew you better."

"What do you mean by that?" Cara demanded.

"I mean — suppose this were for real," Brent answered. And then, as he saw her startled expression, he added brusquely, "Never mind. Forget it. We'll just go on play-acting."

Cara did not know why she suddenly thought of that moment now. Perhaps because it was so at variance with Brent Butler's usual businesslike manner when he was arranging the details of her visit to Soundings. He had been careful to explain — almost as if she had inquired about the other guests at a hotel — that she was to assume her role of fiancée not only for his Uncle Josh but for his young aunt, Susan Evans, and his cousin Paul Rogers. Then he had proceeded to give her a thumbnail sketch of those she would meet.

"My aunt, Sue Evans, is less than ten years older than I am. She's lived most of her life — her married life, that is — in Haiti. Her late husband managed a huge plantation down there, and there's one child, Linda. Then there's my cousin Paul — the perennial college boy type. You'll probably fall in love with him; most women do. But I've never trusted him. He's always looking out for Paul; doesn't care who gets hurt if he wins."

"I guess we'll be pretty well chaperoned then," Cara said demurely, and Brent gave her one of his rare smiles of pure amusement. "But they sound like rather nice people," she added, "in spite of your damning them with faint praise. I don't see why I shouldn't have a good time — while I'm looking out for your uncle's health."

"You'll see," was Brent Butler's enigmatic answer.

Now, as she turned off the highway onto the road which led only to

Soundings, she suddenly felt a touch of fear.

The branching road was winding. It was a tortured road, Cara thought to herself; an unhappy, uncared for pathway, once apparently wide and impressive, now shrinking under the encroachment of bushes and brambles and young trees. She did not quite know what she had expected, but the very sound of a twenty-five-acre estate on Long Island, as Brent described it, conditioned her for a well-groomed establishment. Yet there was no sign of affluence; no gatehouse, no stately stone pillars at the entrance to the road.

Impulsively, Cara drew over to one side where there was space to park. She took out the map Brent had made for her and checked her surroundings. She was not lost; this was surely the road to Soundings.

"Well, I've never visited a really wealthy family before," she murmured aloud. "Maybe this is the way the rich live nowadays." But she wondered nervously what kind of dwelling — there must be a mansion! — awaited her at the end of the neglected road.

Yet even the discouraging approach did not prepare Cara for the house which finally came into view. It was brown, for one thing. Who ever heard of painting a mansion brown? It was a large house, however, and looked lived-in, though there was a vaguely sinister air about it — that dun color! — which increased Cara's uneasiness.

The house stood on a broad, low knoll, brooding, Cara thought, over the cove below. Beyond the inlet Long Island Sound looked placid in the afternoon sun. It was, Cara noted, driving slowly along the gravel road that completely encircled the house, a somewhat misshapen dwelling. The larger section, the main unit, was two and a half stories high, with a slanting roof into which gabled windows had been set. But one end mushroomed into three stories, with a roof that angled its way past the second story and gave the section a top-heavy look. It was as if two houses of different design had been pushed together on that side.

Cara's doubts about the wisdom of taking the job increased. She drew up at the steps which ran the full length of the grass-topped terrace across the entire front of the main section and gazed with trepidation at the house.

Then, somewhat shakily, she turned the handle of the car door and stepped out.

"The die is cast!" she muttered to herself, and then shuddered at her choice of words.

2

CARA never expected to be met by Brent Butler with open arms — literally. But when she brought the convertible to a halt before the chipped terrace of the brown house, he unfolded his long figure from a lounge chair and came down the steps with quick strides. Then, as he caught her in his arms, he said in a clear and carrying voice:

"Carita! Did you have a ghastly trip, my own? Why don't you get that car of yours air-conditioned?" He bent to kiss her, and Cara felt the pleading pressure of his lips before she started to draw away. Brent's arms tightened about her like steel bands. "You dope, we're in full view of the house," he whispered in her ear. "Make with the romance — and make it good!"

Cara had seen no one else around,

but she took his word about the unseen audience. Some time later she was amused to see Brent's face had turned a dull brick-red under the enthusiasm of her responsive kiss. This time he was the one who drew away.

"Overdoing it a bit, aren't you?" he muttered, and then added aloud: "Oh, here you are, Paul! I'm going to make the introductions, but I want it strictly understood Cara is mine, all mine."

"Oh, come now!" A deep, attractive voice spoke just behind her. "Surely a cousinly kiss wouldn't be out of the way?"

"Surely it would!" Brent said sharply. "Cara, may I present Paul Rogers?"

Cara turned and looked with interest at the man whose voice had already intrigued her. He was tall and broad-shouldered. What was it Brent had said about him? "The perennial college boy type?" His white tennis shirt and shorts intensified the bronze of rippling-muscled arms and legs; the sun gilded his hair and made his blue eyes paler.

Cara extended her hand.

"Compromise kiss," murmured Paul with a side glance at his cousin, and lifted the hand to his lips. Even as he released her hand, he contrived to draw her a shade closer. Cara felt herself coloring, and when she looked at Brent, she saw his eyes were narrowed in the oddly disconcerting habit he had — at once calculating and disapproving. Really, she thought, Brent was taking his 'Cara-is-all-mine' ultimatum too seriously.

"Tired?" he asked as they mounted the steps to the terrace overlooking the Sound. "I'll have you shown to your room . . ."

"I'm not a bit tired," said Cara perversely. "I want to watch the sun on the water for a few minutes."

As she had hoped, Cousin Paul remained with them. Cara sank into a big old-fashioned wicker chair, well-cushioned, and he sat on the broad arm of her chair, which creaked under his weight. Brent returned to the lounge chair he had been sitting in when Cara arrived.

A stooped, elderly man approached noiselessly and looked at Brent as if in inquiry.

"Kelty, will you have Miss Merrill's car put in the garage, please," Brent said, "and then bring us something to drink. Cara?"

"I'm dying of thirst," Cara confessed. "I'd adore some iced tea."

"And you can bring me a drink while you're at it," said Paul. "Playing tennis with that half-pint Linda is more of a workout than playing with a pro."

"Iced coffee for me," said Brent, "and whatever kind of sandwiches Mrs. Kelty sees fit to give us. Mrs. Kelty is the cook," he explained to Cara as the man went away. "We are usually vague about afternoon tea," he added, "but Mrs. Kelty always has something on hand, just in case."

"It's a . . . " Cara began, and stopped. She had been going to say 'good', but remembered her debutante status and changed it for the livelier, "a keen custom, I think."

Uncle Joshua, Cara learned, was taking his afternoon nap and would probably not be down until dinner time. She felt a twinge of disappointment. A lot depended upon Uncle Josh. If he took a dislike to her, for instance, she could not stay, whether she was supposedly Brent's fiancée or not. It was Joshua Butler's house, and from all Brent had told her, he was a man of many whims.

She learned more about Uncle Josh as they sat around the small tea table Kelty set up on the terrace. Cara wondered idly why they didn't have the terrace paved. Grass, however neatly trimmed, seemed to her unstable anchorage for a table, or even chairs. One of Joshua's whims, she thought, only half aware of the talk between Brent and Paul. But she started to listen when Paul said:

"I hear Chumley got an offer of half a million for the estate, but Uncle Josh won't say yes and he won't say no."

"Chumley," said Brent to Cara, "is Uncle Josh's lawyer. I suppose," he added sarcastically as he turned to Paul, "Chumley confided this news to you?"

"You don't suppose anything of the sort," Paul retorted good-naturedly. "It was his secretary — Anita-what's-her-name — who told me."

"I shouldn't think you'd stoop to such tactics," Brent said coldly. "You could get the girl fired."

"What Chumley doesn't know won't hurt him," said Paul airily. "On the other hand, information such as I obtained may be useful to us. It's just as well to know what's going on, isn't it?"

"I'd be more interested if you tried to find out the reason for these stomach upsets Uncle Josh has been having lately," said Brent.

Paul shrugged, "It's all of a piece. If Uncle Josh's health is failing, and he changes his will . . . you know that's why he got us all down here . . ."

"I'm afraid this isn't too interesting

for Cara," Brent interrupted.

"Why not?" asked Paul. "If she's going to marry you, I should think she'd be all agog to find out when, if, and what you're going to inherit."

Cara was growing increasingly uncomfortable; she had half decided to go to her room and wait for the dinner bell when a small girl hurtled herself around the corner of the house and up the steps.

"Hi!" she shouted. "Where's Unc' Josh?"

"Resting," said Brent, "and don't make so much noise. You'll disturb him."

"No, I won't," retorted the child. "He 'dores the ground I walk on."

"Who told you that, you monkey?" asked Brent.

"I heard Mrs. Kelty talking," Linda said, losing interest. "I want a sandwich." She leaned past Brent and snatched a tiny cucumber sandwich from the plate on the table.

"Here!" Brent said with mock

alarm. "You're not supposed to eat cucumbers . . . " But Linda had already devoured it in two bites.

"Oh, fiddle-faddle!" she exclaimed.

"Mrs. Kelty's expression," said Brent to Cara. "The child has picked up a whole new vocabulary since she got here a few months ago. When she first arrived she was speaking a *patois* she learned from the natives in Haiti. She was born there and spent all her life on the plantation until now. But where are your manners, Linda? You haven't even spoken to our guest." He took the child's arm and turned her to face Cara; Linda glanced at her indifferently.

"Don't know her," she said.

"Cara, this is Linda Evans," Brent went on imperturbably. "Linda, say something pretty to Miss Cara Merrill."

The child's bright brown eyes traveled over Cara from head to foot. "What a doll!" she said obligingly.

Paul burst into laughter. "That's not one of Mrs. Kelty's expressions;

it's mine!" Still laughing, he caught Linda around the waist and tried to lift her to his knees. But she wretched herself away.

"Keep your hands to yourself!" she said with almost adult sharpness. "You must not touch me. No one must touch me. It is taboo!"

Cara was startled by the outburst. What a strange child! She was wearing a red bathing suit and was small for her age — nine, Brent had told her — and reminded Cara of tales of elves she had read when she was young. Linda's face was definitely elfin. Her straight brown hair swung to her shoulders, framing a pointed chin and large brown eyes below straight bangs. She had a funny nose that curved in at the bridge and a wide mouth, the upper lip very short. It was not an unattractive face, but it was — elfin.

Having freed herself from Paul's grasp, Linda raced away.

"She wouldn't go near the Sound alone, would she?" Cara asked nervously.

"Oh, no!" said Brent. "She has a wading pool of her own. Uncle Josh installed it for her after first exacting a promise she'd keep away from the big pool and the Sound both, unless a grown-up was with her. She wouldn't go back on her word to Uncle Josh; they're real buddies."

"Did I hear my name mentioned?" rasped a voice in the doorway, and the next moment Uncle Josh was being propelled in a wheel chair over the terrace. He was a powerful, thick-shouldered man with a thatch of white hair and bushy white eyebrows which seemed drawn together in a perpetual frown. A light lap robe covered his useless legs.

"We mentioned you only in the kindest way, Uncle Josh," Paul said indolently.

Brent jumped to his feet and waved away the white-coated middle-aged man who was pushing the chair.

"I'll take it, Fred. You get my uncle's pipe. My fiancée has been looking forward to meeting you, Uncle Josh," he said, bringing him over to Cara. "This is my fiancée; Carita — my uncle, Joshua Butler."

"Sit still — sit still," said Joshua irritably as Cara started to rise. "I can see you fine just where you are." He stared up into her face, his eyes narrowing in the same way as his nephew's.

"Fiancée, eh?" he commented. "Sensible-looking girl."

"Why, Uncle Josh, she's a beauty!" Paul protested.

"Did I say she wasn't?" rasped Uncle Joshua. "Any reason beauty and brains can't go together once in a while? But you're like all young men — both of you. Looks are everything, as far as you're concerned. It's only your good luck, Brent, that your girl has looks *and* brains."

"How do you know?" asked Brent, laughing.

"Sticks out all over her," his uncle retorted. "Not a nitwit, like some of those society girls you've brought around before . . . "

"Cara's a society girl," put in Paul mockingly. "Same type as Diane Forbes. Doesn't Diane know about your engagement yet, Brent?"

Uncle Joshua's roar made it impossible for Brent to answer the malicious thrust.

"Hold your rumor-mongering tongue!" he bellowed. Then, patting Cara's arm: "Excuse me, my dear. I'm a patient man, but sometimes . . . " He shook his white head as if words failed him in his effort to explain the provocation he suffered. "Sit next to me at dinner," he said gently.

Then, as he started to turn his chair around, he added tartly: "Where the devil did Fred get to?"

Unthinkingly, her nurse's training getting the better of her, Cara jumped to her feet and started to wheel the chair over to the table. Fred was already in the doorway, but Brent moved more quickly.

"Let Fred do that," he said sharply, and added as an afterthought, "dearest."

As she relinquished the handles of the chair to the man-servant, Cara caught an angry expression in Brent's eyes.

Covered with confusion — she would never, never be able to maintain her masquerade in that house! — Cara sank into the wicker chair she had first chosen. Kelty had cleared away the tea things, and Paul was standing at the edge of the terrace, staring at the Sound. Brent smiled apologetically at Cara and remarked on the beauty of the scene.

"Has anybody seen Linda?"

A tall, forty-ish woman in gray slacks and a green pull-over swung up the steps, a basket with a few roses on her arm.

"Linda was here a little while ago," said Brent. "She snatched a cucumber sandwich and went that-away." He waved his arm in the opposite direction from which the woman had come."

"She'll be back, if only to make her daily plea to be allowed to have her dinner with Unc' Josh," said Paul soothingly.

"Susan, I want you to meet my fiancée, Cara Merrill," said Brent, taking the basket from the woman. "I see you've tracked down quite a few blooms already," he went on, looking down at the scant flowers she had collected.

"The roses are too neglected; they won't do well this year." Susan, very much the sophisticate, bent over Cara's chair and kissed her lightly on the cheek. "Darling, how nice for Brent to find a new fiancée."

"I've never been engaged before!" Brent protested. "Susan, you're trying to create a rift between me and the woman I love." He gave her a small spank as she passed him on the way to a chair.

"A little more respect, please," said Susan, sitting down and crossing her long legs gracefully. "I'm your aged aunt, and I ask you to keep that in mind."

"She's Uncle Josh's half-sister," drawled Paul. "Years and years younger, of course."

"Thank you, Paul," said Susan.

She sank back against the cushions of her deep chair and smiled at Cara. It was a warm, intimate smile, and suddenly Cara felt her heart begin to pound with a heavy measured beat. Her impulse was to jump up and run away; to turn her head so those warm brown eyes could not look at her so searchingly. But this she must not do.

Cara clenched her hands and met Sue Evan's friendly stare with as much composure as she could manage.

"Brent darling, I approve of your choice," Susan said finally. "I'm surprised you were smart enough to pick a girl like Cara Merrill, and even more surprised to find a girl like Cara Merrill would let herself be picked by you!"

"I'll ignore the insult," Brent said.

"You sound as if you had met Cara before."

"But of course I have, darling! We've met, Cara haven't we? You remember me, don't you?"

Cara gave a little sigh. She did indeed remember Mrs. Susan Evans. So the masquerade was over before it had really started!

3

CARA continued to stare at Mrs. Evans as if hypnotized. Brent's aunt had straight brown hair, much like her daughter Linda. But there the resemblance ended. Susan's face was long and thin, in contrast to the wide cheek bones and pointed chin of the little girl. Also, Susan's eyes were not so arresting and were a paler brown than her daughters.

Of course she recognized the woman, Cara thought miserably, as readily as the woman knew her. Susan Evans had been a patient in the hospital some months before when she was recovering from an appendectomy. Ordinarily Cara would not have been called to help out with a patient in a private room, but for a couple of hours one March day she had taken over for the special duty nurse, who was a friend of hers.

In the sheltered intimacy of a private hospital room, nurse and patient quickly got to know each other; Cara thought she could have instantly recognized Susan Evans even in a crowd. But she had been hoping the recognition would not be mutual and, she thought dully, she had hoped in vain. As from a great distance she heard Brent asking warily:

"Where do you think you met my fiancée, Aunt Sue?"

"Funny thing — I can't remember exactly where. But I do know you, Cara. Tell me, where did we meet?"

Cara stole a quick look at Brent. "You seem familiar to me, too," she said hesitantly.

"I imagine you both get around a bit," Paul commented dryly.

"I seem to remember a big place with lots of lights . . . Yet it was quiet . . . And there were flowers . . . "

"I know where it was!" Brent said, and laughed. Cara looked at him in alarm, but at his next words she drew a breath of relief. "You went to one of your numerous charity balls — one Cara had got roped into too, — and you met in the ladies' room!"

Susan and Cara laughed with him; the bad moment was over. But later on Cara saw Brent in the hall and asked anxiously:

"Do you think Mrs. Evans will remember eventually? I did take care of her, you know, when she was in the hospital."

"I doubt very much if Sue will think about it again," Brent said, his eyes narrowing as he looked at her. "After all, a nurse's uniform against the background of a hospital makes almost every girl somewhat anonymous. It's our hard luck you were her nurse. I wish you'd told me."

"But I wasn't!" Cara exclaimed. "I just relieved her regular nurse, and only for a couple of hours."

"Then we're safe," Brent said, and seemed much reassured.

Cara thought about that as she went

to her room to dress for dinner. Uncle Joshua, she had been told, was a martinet on punctuality, especially at mealtime.

Now that Cara thought about Brent's insistence on the masquerade, it seemed odd he took it so seriously. Even if Susan Evans were taken into their secret and learned Cara was a nurse — what difference would it make? Cara liked Mrs. Evans, who appeared to like her. Why did Brent find it necessary to deceive his aunt as well as Uncle Joshua? It was a question which was strangely disturbing and one to which she did not have the answer — yet.

* * *

"My, we're looking blooming this morning!"

Joshua Butler's words were complimentary, and although his tone was gruff he looked indulgent. "I know you and that nephew of mine were dancing until all hours last night," he continued. "I heard you come in at half past three, so you have no right to be out here in the rose garden at eight-thirty in the morning looking as fresh as a Sarabande rose."

"I see you have a Sarabande bush over here in the corner," Cara evaded, looking around at weedy rutted paths and the shredded leaves of each once lovely rose-bush. "I love their orange-red color. Of course your bush should be sprayed and pruned . . . "

"What do you know about taking care of roses?"

"We had a rose garden at home when I was growing up." Cara stopped, reluctant to admit the rose garden had consisted of only six bushes in the back yard of a New York suburb where she had lived when she was very young.

"My wife planted these rosebushes," Joshua Butler said. "I never cared much about them, and after she died I just let them go. It seems to me, young lady, you're trying to get out of telling me where you went last night and what you did. How about it? Will you come clean, as they used to say in the gangster pictures?"

Cara had no intention of telling him about her evening with Brent, which had been satisfactory in a way yet faintly disturbing. Although her 'fiancé' had gone through all the motions for the benefit of anyone who might be at the country club, Cara had the feeling he cared nothing for her personally; that he was only waiting for her to take the first step in checking on his uncle's health.

"I imagine we did what most engaged couples do," she said, smiling as she perched on a garden bench near Joshua Butler's wheel chair. "We danced a little . . . we talked a lot . . . "

"And you stopped somewhere and smooched on the way home."

Cara smiled as if in agreement, but Brent's uncle was mistaken. They had come straight home from the dance, and Brent had said scarcely a word during the entire trip. It would never do, though, to let Joshua Butler discover how unromantic the date had been.

"You're not going to get any spicy details from me," Cara said now. "What I'm interested in is — why were you awake at three-thirty in the morning? Did you have a good book, or were you just checking up on us?"

Joshua Butler's bushy eyebrows drew together as he frowned. "I dislike mentioning my infirmities, but sometimes at night I have occasional aches and pains. Last night I didn't want to take a sleeping pill; I was feeling sort of squeamish. Did you think the seafood cocktail we had at dinner last night was a little too hot?"

Cara assured him truthfully the cocktail sauce, and indeed the whole dinner, had been delicious. She was sure, thinking back on the meal, her host had eaten exactly the same food as everyone else. She felt she owed it to Brent, however, to inquire cautiously of Joshua if he had eaten something strange during the day. The man seemed to hesitate for a moment before answering; then he denied vehemently he had had anything unusual in the way of food.

Cara looked at him with a carefully guileless expression. She did not like what she saw. Yesterday, when she had arrived, his complexion had been healthy and there was even faint color in his cheeks. Today his skin looked sallow and drawn, almost as if he were jaundiced.

Although Joshua Butler's legs were withered from disuse, it was quite obvious he kept the upper half of himself in good physical shape. Indeed, Brent had mentioned that one room at Soundings was specially equipped with parallel bars and other gymnastic devices.

She must find out what his hesitation meant, Cara decided. But before she could ask any further questions Paul Rogers, led by Linda, suddenly rounded the hedge of roses.

"I told you she was out here," the

child said, her big brown eyes so bright they seemed almost to snap.

"Were you looking for me?" Cara asked in astonishment. "Does Brent want me?"

Paul Rogers turned to the man in the wheel chair with a resigned shrug. "What chance has a guy got?" he demanded. "All I wanted to do was show her around this decrepit estate and maybe get a chance to make a good impression. After all, if we're going to have a beauty in the family, I should at least be well acquainted with her."

"Watch your language when you talk about my estate," Uncle Josh said, and although he did not smile, Cara had a feeling this was the usual interchange of insults between himself and Paul.

"I was only going to show her the swimming pool."

"I didn't know you cared about the place. I thought you wanted me to sell."

"If you're not going to take care of

the place, of course you should sell," Paul said firmly, and suddenly the boyish charm Cara had noticed the day before was overlaid by a businesslike manner.

"I haven't yet made up my mind," Joshua Butler said stubbornly, "and nobody's going to rush me. But I gather you've heard about the offer made to Chumley last week . . . "

Cara thought it would be better if she and Linda took themselves out of earshot while the men were discussing business. Paul protested he still wanted to take her on what he called the guided tour, and Cara promised she and the child would not go far away.

Then, as Brent came into the garden and caught the last words, he abruptly vetoed the plan and said he would show his fiancée around himself. However, when he lingered a minute to talk with his uncle, Cara took Linda's hand and drew her away down the path.

It was pleasant, she reflected, to have two handsome young men vying for her attention. It did not matter she was at Soundings under false pretenses. Maybe she was not a debutante; maybe she was simply a nurse between jobs — in a manner of speaking — but anyway, it was fun to find out how the other half lived. And for the moment she did not have to worry about such mundane affairs as paying the rent and stocking the refrigerator.

"You look all starry-eyed," Linda commented. "Is that because you're engaged? Do you like being engaged? Did you have a good time last night? When people get engaged, don't they get married right away? When are you going to get married?"

"My goodness," Cara laughed, "you ask more questions in a minute than I can answer in a day. But thank you for the compliment about my eyes. Of course, when you're in love, the eyes do get shinier."

"I love my Unc' Josh."

"I'm sure you do, but I don't know whether it's made your eyes shinier or not. It seems to me they're as bright as headlights naturally."

Linda nodded soberly. "My Unc' Josh said that, too. Unc' Josh loves me, you know, like I love him. I'm awfully sorry he's sick. But it's all right. I'm going to make him well."

There was complete conviction in the child's solemn voice. Cara looked at her in astonishment. She did not want to tell Linda that the problem of Polio had baffled scientists for centuries and even now required almost constant vigilance and continuing research to keep it in check. It also occurred to her the child might actually be more conversant with her uncle's condition than anyone else, with the possible exception of his man-servant, Fred.

"We all want your Uncle Josh to be strong and well, even if he cannot walk around as the rest of us do," Cara said carefully. "I'm sure your uncle is much better since you and your mother came to visit with him for a while."

Linda shook her head impatiently,

as if she detected an adult's way of discounting what she had said.

"But I *am* going to make him well," she said sharply. "I know how to do it, too. Back home we could get people well any time we wanted to. Of course it's kinda hard up here, because we don't have the same things we had on the plantation. But I'll manage; and I wrote to Mimbo. He can't read himself . . . "

"Hold on a minute. You lost me a while back," Cara interrupted. "Who is Mimbo? Where is back home — Haiti?" There was something frightening about Linda's unchildlike assurance.

Linda picked a rose leaf from a nearby bush and studied it carefully while she explained. Mimbo, Cara learned, had been the overseer of the sugar cane plantation where Linda had lived in Haiti. In the child's eyes he must have appeared old, because she spoke of him with great respect, as well as with affection. But Cara realized that to a little girl of nine, even a man of twenty-five would be a person of years and dignity.

For Linda Evans, it developed as the child talked, the plantation in Haiti was just around the corner from the estate on Long Island. She saw no great difference between the two, just as she saw little difference between Mimbo's cultural background and that of the servants at Soundings. It wasn't necessary for Mimbo to read, Linda said solemnly, because his wife could read everything to him.

Joshua and his nephews were having a lively discussion on the other side of the hedge. And more to keep Linda with her than anything else, Cara asked about Mimbo and the work he had done and was presumably still doing. But the child was not interested in the man's work.

"My Daddy said he was a good man," Linda told her. "I miss my Daddy very much. He wasn't sick at all, you know. If he had been sick even a little while, Mimbo could have saved him. But we woke up one morning and he was gone away forever, Mommy said."

"Your father wasn't sick?" Cara said, echoing the little girl's words. Then suddenly she understood. "You mean your father died of a heart attack?" When Linda nodded, she went on: "I'm sorry, Linda. But why do you say Mimbo could have saved him if he had been sick for a while?"

"Because he could have," Linda said with complete reasonableness. "Mimbo could have used his White Magic, and Daddy would have been all well again. He knows all about White Magic. Mimbo knows about Black Magic, too, but he says that's bad for little girls like me to think about. He says I've got to think about White Magic. Do you think about White Magic when people are sick, Miss Merrill?"

"I don't call it White Magic," Cara said slowly. She wished she did not feel quite so inadequate trying to cope with this strange child. She tried to remember what she knew of Haiti, which she thought someone had once called 'The Land of Voodoo'. If Linda had been brought up in an atmosphere of primitive rituals she might, unknown to her parents, have absorbed certain facts which had become distorted through her immature grasp of them.

"Does your mother know you think so highly of Mimbo?" she inquired.

Linda shook her head. "Mommy doesn't believe in White Magic," Linda said, "but that's 'cause she don't really know about it. If you make a little powder and give it to somebody and say the right things, he'll get all better. Like Uncle Josh will."

"If somebody like your Uncle Josh were ill," Cara said slowly, and found it surprisingly hard to keep her voice steady, "would you give him a powder to make him well?"

"Of course!"

"But maybe he wouldn't take it."

"Unc' Josh will take it," Linda told her confidently. "He promised me he would. Oh," she clapped her hands over her mouth, "I wasn't supposed to tell. You won't tell, will you?"

"I'll make a bargain with you," Cara said, trying not to look as alarmed as she felt. "If you show me the powder *before* you give it to your uncle, I won't tell anybody else. Is it a promise?"

Linda nodded, but Cara was still uneasy.

Would Joshua Butler humor his beloved niece and let himself be dosed with a 'voodoo' potion? Even if she could trust Brent's uncle to be sensible, wasn't it dangerous and unwise to let Linda persist in her belief in a 'magic' she could not understand?

4

"THIS picnic was your idea, not mine," Cara Merrill said as she stretched out on the narrow beach of the cove. The spot was beautiful, the day was warm and sunny, and the placid water of Long Island Sound looked cool and inviting. But Brent Butler, her 'fiancé', looked like a thundercloud and had not said a word for the last fifteen minutes.

"How does it look for two people who are engaged never to be alone?" he demanded, his eyes narrowing as he looked at her. "There's no law says you have to enjoy spending a little time with me, but it looks better to the rest of the household."

"I do enjoy being with you," Cara protested, annoyed that Brent was putting her on the defensive. "But you needn't have snapped my head off when I asked if Linda couldn't come along with us. I'm worried about the child, Brent."

"Worry about me for a change." Suddenly Brent smiled, and Cara caught her breath at his unexpectedly tender look.

By mutual consent they flung off their beach robes and dived into the water. It had been a long time since Cara had been swimming, but she loved the water and easily kept pace with Brent as he swam around the point and followed the coastline. He indicated the boundary of Soundings and, as they reached it, turned back to the small and sheltered cove.

"You know there is a legend that some of our lesser pirates came to the North Shore of Long Island and stashed away some of their treasure," Brent said, vigorously toweling his hair dry. "I like to think the longboats put in at this little cove. Maybe some day we can go exploring."

"I'll go with you any time you say,

sir, but now, since we are alone, don't you think you'd better fill me in on some details that have been puzzling me ever since I arrived here?"

"The water has made your eyelashes stick together in points," Brent observed in an almost impersonal tone. "And you've got your hair wet; I like it better when it's dry and like pale honey, kind of. You're a very beautiful girl, Cara Merrill, but I suppose many men have told you that."

Cara felt a little lost at the sudden turn Brent's conversation had taken. She did not think she would be wise to encourage such a personal discussion; after all, although no one else knew it, she was being paid for her visit to Soundings.

She decided to ask the question that had been in her mind ever since she had met Paul Rogers. As she had hoped, the very mention of Brent's cousin's name created a complete change of atmosphere. In a few terse sentences Brent explained that under the terms of his uncle's present will, Paul Rogers would inherit Soundings. Cash bequests would be made to Susan Evans and a trust fund set up for the child, Linda. He, Brent, would be given only a token legacy since, as Joshua Butler noted in his will, he had a good profession.

During the last six months, however, Brent went on, Uncle Joshua had become dissatisfied with the terms of his will. In the first place, Susan Evans' husband had not been a very provident man, and Uncle Josh was worried about his younger half-sister's future. If Uncle Josh tried to keep up the estate, Susan's cash legacy would be diminished. On the other hand, if he sold Soundings now, Paul Rogers wouldn't get the full amount of the sale.

"It sounds pretty complicated to me," Cara remarked, "but of course it is up to your uncle. Perhaps, aside from wanting to change his will so that Sue Evans will have a larger inheritance, your Uncle Josh finds it too burdensome to keep up an estate of this size. After all, to a man confined in a wheel chair, twenty-five acres is almost useless. All he needs is that terrace."

"I suppose I should have expected you would look at this from a nurse's point of view," Brent said after a moment. "But Uncle Josh bought this place when he was a young man and built this house especially for his bride. There are sentimental reasons he does not want to sell."

"You hired me as a nurse," Cara reminded him. "But, after all, the terms of your uncle's will are no concern of mine."

The better she understood the situation, the better she would understand the problem of his uncle's illness, Brent explained in a rather resentful tone. As far as Brent knew, aside from his polio attack, his uncle had been extraordinarily healthy.

"He never had so much as a headache," said Brent, skipping a stone across the quiet waters of the cove, "until he had called us all together and explained he was about to change his will. Then all at once he began to get these severe attacks of nausea for no apparent reason."

"Do you think your cousin Paul is poisoning your uncle?" Cara said bluntly.

"I didn't say that."

"You must have thought it, and I believe you're wrong. Your Uncle Josh is a strong-willed person; he may be eating something which he knows disagrees with him and not be telling you about it. He may have a stomach condition which requires medical attention. On the other hand, he may be more upset than you realize at the prospect of selling this place; his attacks of nausea may be the result of nervous tension."

"So it's your diagnosis that cousin Paul is completely blameless and I'm a suspicious fellow."

"Don't use the word diagnosis. You hired me to find out what was wrong with your uncle from an observer's point of view; not to make a diagnosis, which I'm not capable of doing in any case."

"I apologize for my choice of words," Brent said dryly. "Why don't we see what Mrs. Kelty put in the lunch hamper and find a pleasanter subject to talk about for a while? Uncle Josh hasn't had an attack since you came."

Cara was about to tell him he was mistaken. The night they had gone dancing at the country club, Uncle Josh had been too upset to take a sleeping pill, he had told her. But since then there had been no further distress; at least Cara had not heard of any. She decided to fall in with Brent's change of mood.

He could be a charming companion. He had worked in strange places, in different countries all over the world, and he had a nice sense of humor. He laughed at some of the difficulties he had encountered because of language barriers or odd customs.

"It's just plain frustrating," he declaimed as he bit into one of Mrs. Kelty's delicious turkey sandwiches, "to work in a place like Thailand. I'm given a job to do and a certain amount of time to do it, whether it's building a bridge or putting in the foundation of a powerhouse. I hire a crew; I have my straw bosses pepped up about the work; the supplies are ready and the great day dawns when we are to start. Then something goes wrong."

"I suppose things always go wrong," Cara said sympathetically. "Even here in America, there is no guarantee that a construction job will proceed smoothly at all times."

"But in this country, if there is a delay, everybody is worried, and everybody works hard to set things right. In the other countries, especially in Thailand or South America, no one is the least concerned about a delay of a week or two weeks or a month. They just don't seem to have any sense of time!"

"Perhaps their philosophy is better than ours," Cara said, stretching out lazily on the blanket she had brought from the house. "The sun is warm, the air is clear, I am so contented with that marvellous lunch I just devoured I could purr like a kitten. Let our problems wait till *mañana*."

"Maybe tomorrow will never come," Brent murmured. He sat down beside her on the blanket and gently stroked her silky hair. Then all at once his fingers reached behind her ear and scratched softly. Cara sat up with a sharp exclamation.

"You're not supposed to tickle me."

"You said you were ready to purr like a kitten. Everybody tickles a kitten behind the ears."

Brent's hand dropped to her shoulder, and his eyes looked deep into hers. For just a moment Cara was tempted to forget the standards she had set for herself — not to encourage any caress which was not required to preserve their status as an engaged couple.

"I changed my mind," she said, getting to her feet abruptly. "I'm going over to that stand of pine on the other side of the cove and look for buried treasure. Want to come along?"

"Don't mind if I do," Brent agreed. "But you needn't be so skittish when we are alone. I don't bite, you know."

Cara pressed her lips together and said nothing. She knew Brent Butler was laughing at her, but she had never been able to think of a caress as casual. Perhaps, she thought as they went toward the grove, if she had really been the debutante she was supposed to be, she could have accepted his attentions as lightly as they were given.

From then on it was a very pleasant afternoon, Cara thought. They talked a lot of nonsense while pretending to search for buried treasure. They raced each other through the blue-gray waters of the Sound and then turned and came back with leisurely strokes. They repacked what Cara called the pitiful remains of the picnic lunch.

And then they stood close together for a moment, looking out at the water as if reluctant to leave. It occurred to Cara that if anyone were watching from the path leading to the Sound, they would certainly present a perfect picture of an engaged couple so much in love they did not even need to talk.

"Hello, you two!" Paul Rogers' hail was so much in line with what she had been thinking Cara could not repress an involuntary start as she turned around. The blond and handsome Paul was standing at the first curve of the pathway, one hand upraised in a salute.

"We're coming." Brent reached down and picked up the picnic hamper. Then, as they started toward Paul, he put his arm around Cara's waist. As she looked at him inquiringly, Brent bent his head in a lover-like gesture and murmured:

"If you demand an audience every time I touch you, I'm sure going to take advantage whenever anyone else is around."

Before she could understand the full import of his words, Brent kissed her lightly on the lips and then grinned at her surprised expression.

"I've been wanting to do that all afternoon, you know. I guess I'm the only man in the world who was ever 'engaged' to a girl he wasn't supposed to kiss in private!"

Paul Rogers was looking down at them with a quizzical smile as they approached. "Don't hurry on my account!" he said, pretending to yawn. "I'm just a messenger boy. Aunt Sue sent me down to call you, Brent. A friend of yours has arrived. Female."

"No friend of mine if she breaks up my afternoon with Carita," Brent said gallantly.

"We were going back anyway," Cara said in an off-hand manner. "We had a lovely afternoon, Paul. The water is just perfect. You should have been . . . " Cara broke off, her face scarlet.

"I should have been with you?" Paul said with a chuckle. "You don't know me very well, Cara. I don't play second fiddle to anyone — not even my Lothario cousin Brent."

Brent apparently had missed the significance of the interchange between Cara and Paul. But he came to a sudden stop at the word 'Lothario' and said sharply to his cousin:

"Just who is waiting for me up at the house?"

"Who would it be?" Paul teased him. And then, as Brent took a menacing step toward him, he backed away. "It's Diane, of course. Diane Forbes, the girl who has scarcely let you out of her sight — when you were in this country, that is — for lo, these many years!"

"Is it someone I should know?" Cara asked.

"No," said Paul grimly. "But you will."

* * *

Diane Forbes was a stunning-looking girl, Cara decided when first she met her. Five minutes later she thought she was also one of the rudest and most unpleasant personalities she had ever known.

Diane's hair was such a dark brown it seemed to be almost black, and it grew in a perfect widow's peak that seemed to accent her beautifully patrician nose. Her chin was small but determined-looking, with just a suggestion of a dimple, and her eyes, although not large, were bright blue and somewhat malicious.

"So you're Cara Merrill," was her greeting. "I couldn't believe it when Sue Evans told me someone had finally snagged our elusive Brent — for the moment, at least. What did you use, my dear? Blackmail?"

It was laughingly said, but Diane Forbes' flashing blue eyes held no hint of laughter. Clearly she had marked Brent for her own, and she had no intention of letting some unknown capture him.

"I didn't use blackmail," Cara

retorted, trying to keep her tone as insolently amused as Diane's had been. "But I must confess I allowed myself to be dazzled." She held out her left hand; the sapphire ring sparkled, and the circle of diamonds shot fire in a most satisfactory way. She had the pleasure of seeing Diane Forbes taken aback momentarily.

But the debutante recovered her poise quickly and turned to Brent, who had been standing by after the introduction, seemingly unperturbed.

"Darling, you don't waste money on engagement rings, do you?" Diane purred. "I seem to remember the sapphire was your grandmother's."

"That's why I love it so much," Cara began hotly, but was interrupted by the entrance of Joshua Butler, wheeled in by Paul Rogers and with Sue Evans walking beside him.

"I heard you were here, Diane," Joshua said, accepting her light kiss on his cheek. "But I don't know who invited you."

"I'll overlook your rudeness, Uncle Josh," Diane said, tapping him reprovingly on the nose, "because I had an invitation. From Sue."

"You twisted my arm, over the phone," Susan Evans commented dryly. "Especially when you heard Brent was here with his fiancée."

"I'm glad you could come," Joshua said hastily. "How is your father, and when is he coming home?"

"Oh, I left Dad up to his ears in red tape and stuff in London, but he should be back next month. Mums, of course, is in Paris — unless she went down to the Riviera after I left . . . "

Cara saw Paul's eyes on her and, although she knew she was being oversensitive, thought he looked at her with pity. She was an outsider here, his glance seemed to say. She could never hope to rival a girl like Diane Forbes, who crossed the Atlantic as casually as others crossed the street and who spoke of London and Paris as if they were neighboring towns. Suddenly Cara remembered her cheap, mean little apartment in Greenwich Village — light years away from this luxurious living room and these wealthy, sophisticated people.

What am I doing here? she asked herself from the depths of the depression that suddenly engulfed her.

5

THE mood persisted all through dinner. Cara Merrill could find no opening by which to enter the conversation which swirled around and over her as if, she thought to herself, she were the original invisible woman. She fixed a small, politely interested smile on her face and learned how bored Diane had been in Rome; how much money a couple she had met had lost at Monte Carlo; how "perfectly fascinating" it had been to watch a movie company on location in Greece.

Everyone else seemed to consider Diane's gay account of the latest doings in the 'jet set' as interesting and, in some strange way, important. Cara looked around the table and saw all the people there with new eyes: Joshua Butler, white-haired and patrician; Sue

Evans, stunning in a smart black dinner dress, with her hair piled high on her head; Diane in blue chiffon, vivacious and charming; Brent and Paul in white dinner coats, laughing at Diane and trying to make her angry with sharp comments born of long and intimate friendship.

It was really a delightful dinner party, Cara thought bitterly. The only trouble was — she had no part in it.

At one point Cara did try to enter into the conversation a little bit. Diane was talking about Barcelona and a "simply fabulous" luncheon she had attended.

"I suppose the most popular matador was throwing the bull," said Paul, laughing.

"He was my escort," Diane admitted. "But he was a difficult person, frightfully intense. I really thought it was better to go back to Paris right away, and I was sorry, too."

"Sorry to leave the matador?" asked Brent.

"Sorry to leave the wonderful Spanish food, darling," Diane said with a smile that excluded everyone else at the table.

It was then that Cara turned to Susan and asked with a show of interest: "Speaking of food — you must have had some wonderful native dishes during the time you lived in Haiti."

Sue Evans looked surprised. "It was good. I never had anything to do with the shopping or preparation, of course."

"Of course not," Cara said, feeling sorry she had mentioned it. Sue added quickly:

"But there was one thing I always had served with the cocktails. There's a large green banana the natives slice thin and fry until its crisp. Quite a different taste."

"I've had them," Paul put in. "Remind me of potato chips, sort of."

But the subject held no interest for Diane Forbes; she leaned over and patted Joshua Butler's arm.

"Dad told me to give you his best," she said in a low voice. "He said not to buy — oh, I forgot the name of the stock — "

"Never mind," Uncle Joshua smiled at her indulgently and then looked sharply at his nephews. "I'm staying out of the market for a while until I make up my mind about a new will. Anyway, I'll talk with your father when he gets back. D'you think he'll be home *early* next month?"

Diane shrugged. "It's awfully hard to keep track of parents, Uncle Josh."

"Or parental uncles," Brent said with a smile. "Maybe your Dad will be here for our annual fireworks at the country club on the Fourth."

"Do they have a real old-fashioned celebration?" Cara asked. "With pink cotton candy and popcorn?"

Paul looked at her oddly. "I never noticed the popcorn," he said flatly.

"I'm sure you noticed the old-fashioneds, my lad." Diane laughed.

"Try one made with vodka sometime. It's quite different from a Scotch old-fashioned. But speaking of fireworks, you should have seen the display Dad put on when he heard I'd ordered a topless bathing suit!"

Cara Merrill grimly concentrated on her dessert. She did not know whether Diane had purposely talked over her head or not, but she thought she could detect a feline smirk of satisfaction on the debutante's beautiful face as Paul and Brent both started a lively discussion of the more scandalous aspects of high fashion.

After dinner was over, Cara breathed a sigh of relief. Surely conversation would be more general when they got back to the living room. Brent took her arm, and Cara leaned back and looked up into his face with what she considered the properly adoring gaze of an engaged girl. Brent, leaning down so that his lips brushed her forehead briefly, murmured:

"Diane's slightly terrific, isn't she?

She's always in the middle of everything; she knows everybody and goes everywhere. Yes — she's quite a girl!"

Cara allowed herself to be brought over to the chintz-covered sofa. She smiled at Brent as if he had just said something very romantic and as if she were answering in kind.

"I am overwhelmed. Do I gather that you two were 'going steady' before I came into the picture?"

"I suppose so," Brent said carelessly. "We grew up in the same crowd, you know — went to the same dances and all that sort of thing. Lately, she's sort of managed to be around, no matter where I was. Why, would you believe it — she even turned up at a job I was on in New Mexico!"

"I'd believe it," said Cara, but her tone of voice was lost on Brent.

"Another time, I was walking down the main drag in Rangoon — and there was Diane. She said she just happened to be passing by. Yes, she's quite a girl!"

"Since you're under constant surveillance," Cara commented, "I wondered you dared to say you were engaged to anyone else. Why didn't you tell me there was a Diane Forbes in your life?"

Brent looked at her in surprise. He started to answer her and then checked himself, his eyes narrowing. Finally he asked:

"What difference does it make? Why should you care whether I've been going around with Diane — or anyone else? You know our engagement is phony."

"I only wanted to remind you of it," Cara said sweetly. "For a while this afternoon, I thought you might be forgetting, or taking advantage of my situation."

"You can sure make a mountain out of a molehill," Brent started to say when he was abruptly shushed by Paul.

"Diane has come back with the best collection of French songs we've ever heard," he said, leading her over to the grand piano. "And she's just dying to entertain us, aren't you, pet?"

"No, I'm not," Diane said, wrinkling her nose at him. "But I will sing some of them — for Brent."

Cara thought her 'fiancé' might have shown a little more reluctance in going over to the piano; she had no choice but to get up and follow him. Susan Evans was pressed into service to improvise an accompaniment, and again Cara felt as if she had vanished into thin air.

"Come and sit over here near an old man," Joshua Butler commanded. Cara sank into the armchair next to him gratefully. It was obvious both Paul and Brent were not getting farther away from Diane than the other side of the piano.

Then, with an imperious gesture of silence, Diane began to sing. Her voice was light and true, apparently well trained, and her songs were in French, which she seemed to know as perfectly as she knew English.

The only trouble was, Cara thought, miserably settling back in her chair, she did not understand a word of French — and everyone else did. As Diane rattled through a chorus and then slowed up to make each word count in what was evidently the 'punch line', both Paul and Brent listened with evident delight and then roared with laughter.

Beside Cara, Joshua Butler gave a deep chuckle and then asked in a low rumble, "Speak French?" When Cara shook her head, his eyes twinkled and he said lightly: "Maybe it's just as well. You look too sweet and innocent to understand these French parodies."

Diane Forbes had quite a collection of new songs, which her audience enjoyed to the hilt. Cara decided there was nothing to do but again fix a stiff little smile on her lips and sit through the recital. Perhaps the time would come when she could gracefully plead a headache and go to her room.

She did not know when she became

conscious of Joshua Butler's breathing. To anyone else, it would probably not have been noticeable, but to Cara, trained to hear a difference in ordinary regular breathing and the deep, straining breaths the man in the wheel chair was now trying to conceal, the effort he was making was quite obvious. Then, looking at him closely, she saw his skin had again taken on a sallow, yellowish tinge such as she had noticed when they were out in the rose garden.

Cara waited until Diane reached the end of the song, politely joined in the laughter, then stood up abruptly.

"Uncle Joshua and I want to thank you, Diane, but now we must ask to be excused," she said, assuming an assurance she did not feel. She put her hands possessively on the wheel chair. "I'm taking you to your suite," she said.

Joshua Butler looked at her, his eyes narrowing like his nephew's, and for a moment Cara was afraid he was going to contradict her. But all at once he smiled and nodded.

"Don't let me break up the concert," he said as Susan started to get up from the piano, "I'll have Cara call Fred Bates when we get to my quarters and send her back to join the party. Now, all of you join me:

"'Merrily we roll along, roll along, roll along,
Merrily we roll along . . .
O'er the deep blue sea.'"

Relieved to hear the homely English phrases, Cara too joined in and wheeled her host down the central hall and through a long corridor to his rooms in one wing of the sprawling house. The room she brought him into was a combination study-library, with three book-lined walls and a fourth of floor-length windows looking toward the Sound. There was a great mahogany desk and a chair of red leather which evidently had been specially made for the invalid.

"Press the button on the desk," Joshua Butler commanded, "and get Bates in here. Then you go on back to the party."

"I have a slight headache," Cara demurred. "Truly, I'd rather go up to my room. But I'm worried about you. Don't you think you'd better lie down? Is there something I can get you?"

"You're a sharp one," Uncle Joshua said, and Cara was relieved to see his color was much better. "I felt a little squeamish there for a few minutes; the room seemed close, stuffy, and I couldn't get my breath. But I'm all right now."

"This is the second time you've told me you felt squeamish after dinner," Cara reminded him. "Yet the dinners are wonderful. Unless you ate something strange for lunch . . . ?"

"Chicken and a glass of milk; I wasn't hungry," Uncle Josh said as if dismissing the incident. "Oh, here you are, Fred. Now we can let Miss Merrill get back to the others."

Cara knew she would have to go, but she couldn't resist saying: "Don't you think you'd better call your doctor? Maybe he could give you something that would soothe your stomach . . . "

"NO!" Joshua Butler's roar was loud and angry. "I won't have a doctor in this house. I had five doctors when I got this thing thirty years ago, and not one of them did me a blamed bit of good. There's nothing the matter with me, but if there was I'd rather ask Linda to send for her witch doctor — Mumbo-Jumbo, or whatever his name is — than some young squirt with a lot of fancy letters after his name."

"That's not fair!" Cara said, forgetting she had no right to argue with her host. "Doctors today are dedicated to the premise you can *keep* well; you needn't be sick. But you've got to give them a chance . . . "

The silver-haired Fred Bates, standing

behind his master's chair, shook his head warningly, and Cara suddenly realized she was speaking out of turn. She managed to force a smile and said, by way of apology:

"My godfather was a doctor. I think of him whenever a doctor is mentioned. Anyway, you know best. I'm glad you're feeling better. Good night, Mr. Butler."

"No harm done," Joshua said, genial once more. "You couldn't know how I feel about the profession. Good night, Cara."

Brent was waiting in the main hall, and he looked anxiously at her as she came up to him. In the living room, she could hear the others talking; Diane had apparently come to the end of her repertoire.

"Is Uncle Josh all right? What was the matter?"

"I don't know, Brent, and I'm worried. I noticed he was breathing unevenly and he looked sick. But he seems all right now. I forgot what you'd told me and said he should see a doctor."

"And got chewed out properly, I'm sure," said Brent.

"That doesn't matter. What does matter is — what gives your uncle these sudden attacks? The dinner was delicious; anyone in normal health could eat it with enjoyment. Your uncle told me what he had for lunch — cold chicken and milk. Yet suddenly, an hour after dinner, he is nauseated and can't get his breath. He calls it feeling 'squeamish'. He *should* see a doctor, Brent. If he eats only the best of food . . . "

"He had a highball before dinner," Brent said suddenly.

"Does he usually have a drink before dinner?"

"Occasionally. I've never known it to bother him before."

"Then it doesn't seem logical it would upset him hours later . . . "

"I suppose not." Brent was staring at the wall behind her head with unseeing eyes. "But this afternoon it was Paul who mixed the highball and brought it to Uncle Josh. It looked like Scotch and soda. But I don't know what was in it."

Cara felt chilled by his words. There was no doubt about it: Brent believed his cousin was poisoning Uncle Josh!

6

"A GARDEN is a lovesome spot," quoted Paul Rogers, leaning over the hedge behind the bench where Cara Merrill was sitting, contemplating the neglected bushes before her. She jumped at the sound of his voice close to her ear.

"Sorry," said Paul. "I didn't mean to scare you. I was about to parody that beautiful poem with a line of my own, to wit: especially when said garden is adorned with a lovesome girl."

"That's not an improvement on the original poem," said Cara. "It doesn't fit the meter, either."

"Criticism, criticism, criticism! The way of the poet, like that of the transgressor, is hard," said Paul. "May I come in?"

"If you like — it's not my garden," Cara said primly.

Paul leaped over the low-growing and, if truth must be told, seedy-looking hedge. "I find myself unable to resist your warm invitation," he murmured. "Now if you will add, 'won't you sit down?' — "

"Won't you sit down?" said Cara obediently, and moved over to make room on the little wrought-iron bench, its peeling green paint making it as forelorn in appearance as the rest of the garden.

"Whole place gone to wrack and ruin, hasn't it?" asked Paul cheerfully. "Should be dug up and grass-seeded."

"How can you say such a thing about a garden of roses?" Cara turned to face him indignantly.

"What roses?" demanded Paul. "What stormy eyes you have, my sweet. When you're mad as hops, I mean, as of now."

"There are some fine rosebushes here. The Sarabande over there, and the Crimson Glory — I'm sure that's what it is — and all those Grandifloras can be restored with a little care and proper feeding."

"The care and feeding of decrepit rosebushes is not a subject in which I shine," murmured Paul. "Are you, by any chance, a rose-grower's daughter?"

Cara laughed. "My knowledge of rose-growing is lately acquired," she confessed. "The few bushes we had at home hardly serve to qualify me as an expert. But since I came here, this neglected rose garden has been a kind of challenge. I'd like to nurse it back to health." Then, fearful that the mention of nursing might rouse Paul's suspicions of her as a butterfly-debutante, she added hurriedly: "I've been reading up on roses in the library here. I understand Uncle Josh Butler's wife had this garden planted, and I found a whole corner of the library devoted to books on rose-growing. She must have loved this poor old garden of hers."

"Your face," said Paul, "is glowing like a rose. I wish I could arouse such enthusiasm for me."

"Don't be silly." Remembering suddenly that she was supposed to be engaged to Brent Butler, Cara spoke shortly and changed the subject.

"I wonder if I could borrow the gardener's tools and fix this place up?" she said.

"There's no regular gardener," explained Paul, "just a touring landscape artist who comes by occasionally to mow the lawn. But there's a tool shed and, for all I know, it's bulging with hoes and rakes. Shall we investigate?"

"Wait a minute," said Cara, as Paul started to rise. "I've got a list here of things I'll need. I copied it out of a book a while ago." She reached into the pocket of her red long-shorts and brought out a crumpled piece of paper with an itemized list.

Smoothing it out, she read it aloud: "Hoe; hand cultivator; pruning shears; trowels; spading fork; iron rake; hand sprayer."

"There ought to be some or all of

these things around," said Paul, "or we can persuade Uncle Josh to buy them for us. I'm appointing myself your helper, you know."

"Oh, I wouldn't want to impose on your time," said Cara hastily. "Aren't you busy?"

"Well, I do have some spare time," grinned Paul. "*That's* when I'll lend a hand. Meanwhile, let us toddle off to the tool shed."

Cara, walking beside him to a cluster of small buildings some distance in the rear of the house, wondered if she had been wise to undertake the rose garden project. She was Brent's debutante fiancée, wasn't she? Did it look a little strange for a girl in her situation — supposedly in love with a highly eligible young man — to be spending hours and hours digging around rose-bushes, especially in the company of Brent's attractive and obviously admiring cousin? How had it come about? she wondered. How had it happened that Paul Rogers was involved with her in the project, which she had planned merely as a kind of leisure time activity for herself alone?

"You'll have to watch your step when you begin handling weed killers and sprays and other such poisonous stuff," Paul said, as he pushed open the unlocked door of the shed. "You'll need some, I suppose. There may even be some in here."

His mention of poison jolted Cara most unpleasantly. Uncle Josh's stomach upset had followed a high-ball Paul had mixed for him the afternoon before, Brent had said. "I don't know what was in it!" he told her, plainly intimating that Paul had given his uncle poison.

The thought brought Cara to a standstill at the door of the shed.

"What's the matter?" asked Paul. "You're afraid there may be rats about? Or maybe skunks?"

"Of course not." Cara recovered herself and followed Paul into the shed. "It does seem to me, though, a place full of tools and possibly poison" — she stammered as she pronounced the word — "ought to be kept locked with a child on the premises. Linda wanders about so . . . "

"Linda lived on a half-wild plantation in Haiti. I think she has a good idea what insect sprays and such are all about. She's a knowing youngster."

"All the same . . . " Cara was beginning when Paul interrupted her.

"Anyway, I don't see any poisons around, do you?" He had scarcely glanced around the shed; how did he know there were no poisons unless he had been there before? Cara wondered. She opened a cupboard door and peered at the shelves. They were empty.

"Oh, come on," said Paul impatiently. "I'm sorry I mentioned poisons; forget it." He moved close to her, put one arm around her waist and closed the cupboard door with his other hand. At that moment a shadow darkened the shed doorway.

"Hi!" Brent's voice was cool,

apparently undisturbed. Cara looked over her shoulder; her eyes met his narrowed ones.

"We were looking for poison," she stammered.

"Indeed," said Brent politely. "Have you a victim in mind?"

Paul Roger's laugh sounded hollow in Cara's ear. "We were looking for something to kill the weeds in the rose garden," he explained after a slight pause. "Cara is determined to rehabilitate it."

"I see," said Brent.

Paul had hastily dropped the arm he had around Cara's waist, and she herself had stepped away from him. For an awkward moment nobody said anything.

"Well," Brent said at last, "I was looking for Cara, and Linda told me she had seen you and Paul" — he smiled at her, but it was a cold smile — "going in this direction. I wanted to ask you — and Paul, of course — if you'd like to go to the Aqueduct races this afternoon. Diane is mad about racing."

"That flagpole isn't very high, is it?" said Cara, as they were passing the plaza at the grandstand entrance at Aqueduct. Cara had at first thought of refusing to join the party. Since Diane's likes and dislikes seemed to carry a great deal of weight with Brent, let them enjoy the races without her! But she had never been to Aqueduct, and the outing promised to be alluring, Diane notwithstanding. Everybody had been in a joyous mood on the drive to the track; she was glad she had come after all. But when Diane hooted with laughter at her remark about the flagpole, she reddened with embarrassment.

"What you don't know about racing, darling!" purred Diane after her laughter subsided. "That's not a flagpole. That's the furlong pole where Man o' War began his winning drive in a 1920 race, in what was considered by many the greatest effort of his career."

"Man o' War was a horse?" asked Cara.

"Catch me, somebody; I'm fainting!" screamed Diane. "She wants to know if Man o' War was a horse!"

Paul patted Cara's shoulder. "Don't mind her," he consoled her. "She thinks anyone who doesn't follow horse racing is retarded. This track we're at is the new Aqueduct. The old one, where Man o' War won his spectacular victory, setting a record, was demolished, and this pole was preserved and set up here. Commemorates a race and a horse that made racing history."

"Thanks, Paul," said Cara gratefully as they followed Brent and Diane, who were walking ahead by now. "I suppose I did sound stupid."

"Nothing of the kind," retorted Paul. "If anyone in this party is stupid, it's Diane. She may know a lot about racing, but can she identify a Sarabande rosebush?" He squeezed Cara's arm, and she smiled.

"You're kind," she told him, and then felt her heart chilling as she realized that Paul — this *kind* Paul — had mixed a drink for Uncle Josh last night that *might* have contained poison! With a definite effort she put the thought aside. She was on a joyous outing; well, then, she would enjoy it!

The party had arrived early, had had lunch in the clubhouse, bought tickets on the daily double, lost on either the first or the second race or both, and watched the running of each race in succession, using the binoculars Brent had brought in turn. Diane made a great show of reading the past performance charts of the horse in each race, solemnly selected the winner and found herself mistaken.

"I'm afraid I'm jinxed today," she said once, looking at Cara.

"Well, it certainly isn't your day," said Brent cheerfully, and Cara could have hugged him. He wasn't sympathizing with Diane! That showed he didn't really love her, didn't it?

But what difference does it make she chided herself the next moment. He isn't in love with me, either!

When the ninth race had been run and they were walking toward Brent's car in the vast parking lot, Diane suddenly announced that she wanted to visit the harness racing track that night.

But Brent flatly refused. "You know how Uncle Josh feels about having everyone home for dinner," he said. "If we'd made arrangements before we left, it would be different."

"You could telephone," said Diane stubbornly.

"No," said Brent. "Uncle Josh doesn't make many rules. The few he sets we ought not to break."

"How idiotic," muttered Diane. "What difference can it possibly make to him whether or not we're on hand when the roast chicken or whatever is set on the table?"

"Uncle Josh has a right . . . " began Brent. But Diane, suddenly smiling, climbed behind the wheel of Brent's car as they reached it.

"I want to drive," she said childishly. "I feel like driving."

"Suit yourself," Brent told her, obviously still annoyed at Diane's behaviour. For several miles Diane, who was an expert driver, kept the car at a normal speed. Then suddenly she let it out and they began zooming along, passing cars at points where warning signs were posted and laughed at Brent's protests.

"We don't want to be late for dinner!" Diane's airy voice floated back to Cara, sitting beside Paul in the rear. "I'm only trying to please Uncle Josh!"

"This isn't a hot-rod!" yelled Brent. "We'll be arrested for speeding. Slow down, Diane, honey."

Tantalizingly, Diane did slow down occasionally; then when she suspected Brent was about to seize the wheel, she speeded up again. Cara tried to carry on a conversation with Paul, hoping to show Diane that she was indifferent to her antics, but her efforts were doomed to failure. Diane deliberately crossed to the oncoming traffic lane as she saw another car approaching, and swerved just in time to avoid a collision by the slightest of margins.

"Well, we made it." Diane grinned maliciously at Brent as she turned into the driveway at Soundings and drew up in front of the house. "Won't Uncle Josh be pleased!"

Nobody made any reply. Even Brent stalked by, his face set, and went upstairs to change for dinner. Cara caught up with him on the stairs.

"Don't upset your uncle," she warned softly. "He was sick yesterday, remember."

"Don't worry. It will be dinner as usual," Brent assured her. "But I can't imagine what got into Diane. She's really a sweet girl."

Cara wanted to say, "So I noticed," but she refrained. After all, Diane was Brent's problem and, for all she knew, the girl he loved. She, Cara, was merely a nurse, brought into the household to watch over Joshua Butler. She had no reason to feel hurt that Brent should find Diane fascinating; perhaps in a way he enjoyed these erratic manifestations.

All the same, Cara was thinking as she slipped a green and white plaid nylon frock over her head, he doesn't deserve the treatment he's getting from Diane. And I don't know why he puts up with her! She yanked the zipper on her dress so hard it stuck, and it took several minutes of patient manipulation to straighten it out, so that she was nearly late for dinner after all.

After dinner, an old friend of Uncle Josh, who lived nearby, came in to play chess, a game at which Joshua had become expert during his years in a wheel chair. Cara found herself alone on the terrace with Brent, all the others having gone to observe the night sky through a telescope which Joshua called one of his 'toys'.

Cara and Brent talked guardedly about Joshua Butler's health, and Brent asked her, point-blank, if she had any clue as yet to the unpredictable upsets he had been experiencing in recent weeks.

"I hope you didn't take seriously what I suggested about the highball Paul gave him yesterday," he said after a while. "But there's something about Paul that worries me, though I can't say what it is. I hope you're not falling in love with him."

"Of course not!" Cara flared hotly. "What you saw in the tool shed this morning was just — just — "

"I understand." Brent's tone was flat. "However, I think it would be better, all around, if you didn't spend too much time alone with Paul."

Cara was so furious she could not trust herself to answer. Was Brent accusing her of leading Paul on, of taking advantage of her situation at Soundings to win a husband who would inherit wealth? Or was he warning her against a man he feared might be a poisoner?

7

PERHAPS it was the memory of how Brent was trying to order her life which made Cara particularly cordial to Paul the next morning. She had gotten up early and on a sudden impulse asked Kelty about weed killer when he served the poached eggs. To her great surprise she found that he had a nice supply of it carefully put away in the cellar.

"After the mistress died, I thought it shouldn't be laying around in the tool shed," the man of all work explained. "Mr. Joshua didn't have no interest in the roses, so I didn't do anything. But if you want me to help you, miss, I could spare a few hours this morning."

"No," Cara said, softening her refusal with a smile. It was really extraordinary how many people wanted to help her restore the rose garden.

"I'd be grateful if you'd get the weed killer from the cellar and give it to me." And then, on a sudden impulse, she added, "I was going to ask Mr. Paul if he couldn't do something about the swimming pool. Perhaps you could help him with that, Kelty."

"That's easy," Kelty said with a complete lack of enthusiasm. "Mr. Paul knows how to do it by himself. There's some cleaner for the pool down the cellar, too; I'll bring that up with the stuff for the weeds."

When Cara finally set out for the rose garden, she not only carried the bulky packages of weed killer and pool cleaner but also a spray gun, gardening gloves and, at Kelty's suggestion, a pair of goggles. When she went upstairs to get the goggles, she noticed Diane's door was still tightly closed. Evidently early rising was not one of Diane Forbes' virtues. She had not seen Brent or Paul, either, but they might have gone to have breakfast with Uncle Josh in his room, as he sometimes requested them to do.

"Lord of the manor stuff, you know," had been Paul's disparaging comment. "But I suppose the poor old guy has to feel needed, even if it's only a matter of giving orders to a couple of nephews who don't really give a darn."

Cara was surprised at Paul's understanding of the problem facing a man in a wheel chair. In the back of her mind as she went into the rose garden was the hope that, if she tried to restore it even in a small way, she might encourage Joshua Butler to become interested in rehabilitating the whole estate.

And if that is contrary to dear Brent's plans for the future, Cara told herself, working the spray gun with unnecessary vigor, then it's just too bad. He ought to worry less about poisoning and put his mind instead on something constructive for his uncle, such as occupational therapy.

Only a few minutes later, Paul

came into the rose garden dressed in Bermuda shorts. He was delighted she had obtained the weed killer and again offered to operate the gun. But Cara pointing out she had also been able to get some cleaner for the pool, suggested he make that his particular project.

"If you know how, that is," she said teasingly.

"I know how to do it," Paul said at once, "but I only work under supervision. I'll drain off the slimy business in the bottom of the pool, but then when I'm ready to clean it out and put in fresh water, you've got to be sitting right on the rim or it's no go."

"I have my own project here with the roses," Cara started to protest. But then, as Paul folded his arms and took up his stance with the evident intention of not budging a step, she relented.

"Oh, all right; go on and get busy with your draining. I'll stop as soon as I use up the spray I already have in the gun."

Paul disappeared down the path which led to the swimming pool and Linda's wading pool — both only a short distance away, although out of sight. She herself continued to spray, trying as best she could to keep the weed killer off the rosebushes. If Kelty really wanted to help, she would tell him to begin by edging the paths and removing the weeds that had sprung up where the gravel was thin. Perhaps Uncle Josh could be persuaded to get a fresh load of gravel and then, if she had any success at all with her efforts, the garden should look quite attractive.

There was a hissing sound which, for a moment made her think she was still working the spray gun. When it was repeated, however, she turned to see Linda Evans, her small face a picture of woe, peering at her around the corner of the hedge.

"Why the secrecy, Linda?" Cara asked gaily. "Come on and talk with me while I dig up a little around this bush. We have to loosen the dirt so, when it rains again, the roots of the bush can get a nice long drink of water."

The diminutive figure of the little girl, dressed in the briefest of sun suits, came toward her. "Where's Paul?" she demanded. "I saw him come out here to talk to you."

"He went over to the swimming pool. Why? Don't you like your cousin Paul?"

"I want to talk to you alone," Linda said solemnly, her brown eyes looking even larger than usual in her elfin face. "I had a letter from Mimbo."

"Oh!" Cara sat back on her heels and gave this statement the serious attention it deserved. "What did Mimbo say?"

Linda shook her head with an almost adult air of disappointment. "He said he couldn't tell me how to make White Magic just in a letter. He said it might not even work all the way up here. He said" — and Linda's voice faltered — "I wasn't big enough to do the Magic all by myself."

Cara recognized how difficult it was for Linda to keep from crying as she repeated the dreadful words. Although she deplored the child's interest in the primitive rituals of Haiti, Linda would probably outgrow her absorption in time, and secretly Cara applauded Mimbo for his firm stand on the subject, even while she wondered what harmless substitute plan she could offer to interest the child. It was Linda herself who unexpectedly supplied the answer.

"I don't need Mimbo to tell me," she said defiantly. "If I just had two feathers from a chicken — you burn them — " she told Cara importantly, "and a lizard that's all dried up . . . "

"This is the wrong part of the country for lizards," Cara said, hoping the difficulties of compounding the magic formula might prove insurmountable. Then, as Linda's face fell, she added: "But why don't we go and ask Paul if he knows where we could find a lizard?"

"I don't want to tell nobody but you."

"We won't tell him anything," Cara said firmly, "except that you are interested in lizards. *Anybody* might inquire about lizards . . . "

Reassured, Linda put her hand in Cara's, and they walked the short distance to the pool. It had been a nice one; it was long and narrow and set against a background of sturdy Scotch pines. The concrete of the edging needed repair and the paint was worn off. Yet it would not take much effort to make it look better. Paul was in water up to his ankles, cleaning out the drain and tossing the wet mass of leaves and sticks and other debris up on the rim by the handfuls.

Lizards, dried or otherwise, were about the one thing he had not found in the drain, Paul assured them. He asked Linda if she would settle for dead beetles, of which there were quite a few. After a few seconds of deliberation, Linda decided this might be a solution. She went over to the mucky pile and began looking through it with interest, and Cara smiled at him gratefully.

"I don't suppose I should ask why lizards?" Paul said, perching on the rim.

"You suppose right," Cara said, sitting beside him.

"'Yours not to question why'. It's Linda's project, and I'm just trying to help her out. Not to change the subject, but what are you going to do about the bottom of the swimming pool? Don't you need a broom or a shovel or something?"

"I was about to go up to the house and ask Kelty . . . well, whom have we here? Lord Chesterfield, I presume?"

Cara looked over her shoulder and blinked in surprise. Brent was standing there, dressed for the city in a lightweight summer suit and a white shirt and a tie. There was no doubt about his destination; he was obviously about to take off for New York. He stood looking at Cara and Paul sitting on the rim of the emptying pool and at the child Linda, who was rapidly transferring most of the mud Paul had taken from the drain to her own arms and legs. He said curtly:

"Diane has to go back to the city this morning, and I said I'd drive her in."

"I thought this was a little too quiet for your friend Diane," Paul said with a shrug.

"She'll be back," Brent assured him. "But I thought I might as well drive her in; I want to see Chumley anyway. I'll come back by train."

"Well," Cara said uncertainly, "tell Diane goodbye, then, and have a good time while you're in the big town."

"I thought you might come out to the car and say goodbye yourself," Brent said coldly.

Paul suddenly chuckled. "I think he wants to kiss you goodbye, Cara darling," he said in a mocking tone.

Cara scrambled to her feet, pink with embarrassment. Of course she should have offered to bid her fiancé a fond farewell without prompting from either man. But for the last few hours she had forgotten she was supposed to be engaged to Brent Butler.

"Could be I'm jealous," she muttered, in an attempt to cover up. "Anyhow, there's no need for me to go around to the car. I'll come with you as far as the rose garden."

She linked her arm with Brent's until they were at a safe distance and out of sight of the swimming pool.

"You almost blew the whole thing up that time," Brent said, his voice edgy. "And I thought I told you to keep away from Paul."

Cara faced him with flashing eyes. "Look here, Brent Butler, I'm getting a little sick of this masquerade. You brought me out here because your uncle had been having attacks of nausea, and you have hinted more than once that someone, perhaps Paul, was trying to give him poison. But your uncle is not a young man, Brent, and naturally he cannot live a normal life in a wheel chair. You must expect that he would have an occasional stomach upset. As for Paul poisoning him, that's just absurd."

"Do you want to chicken out of the deal?" Brent demanded.

"No, I don't. Not right now, that is. I like your uncle, and I want to be perfectly sure in my own mind everything is okay. Oh, darling!" Cara threw her arms around his neck with a sudden violent display of affection.

"I'll miss you every minute," she assured him, and then added in a fierce undertone: "Kiss me as if you meant it. Diane is coming into the rose garden."

Brent responded instantly, and as they drew away Cara had the satisfaction of seeing the brunette's blue eyes darken angrily. Her goodbye to Cara was very brief, and she and Brent disappeared in the direction of the car without delay.

Cara picked up her small trowel and dug at the earth around the rosebush with renewed vigor. Perhaps Brent was regretting his plan to have her pose as his fiancée. Well, when he came back from New York, she would tell him she was ready to call the whole thing off at any time. Certainly she did not have to stay where she wasn't wanted!

Late in the afternoon, Joshua Butler sent his manservant, Fred Bates, to ask Cara if she would have dinner with him on the terrace at seven o'clock. Mrs. Evans and Paul were not having dinner at home, Fred explained, and Linda would eat with Mrs. Kelty at an earlier hour. Cara was a little worried about this tête-à-tête dinner with Uncle Josh. Had he discovered she was there under false pretences? Well, if he had, there was nothing to do but confess and pack up and leave.

But Uncle Josh had something else on his mind, Cara discovered before they had even finished the iced melon that was on the table when they sat down.

"Kelty tells me you're really going to do a job on that rose garden," he began, after he had complimented her on her green chiffon frock. "I didn't know young girls these days took an interest in such things. I thought they were all like that flighty Diane Forbes, whose father doesn't know what country she's in half the time."

"I've always liked roses," Cara said, deliberately evading any comment on Diane. "They are such beautiful flowers, and they respond so well to a little attention. I'm going to enjoy working in the garden, if you don't mind, I mean."

"Mind?" Uncle Josh's bushy eyebrows shot up in astonishment. "Of course I don't mind. Just tell me what you need, and I'll see that you have it. I hear you've got my nephew Paul working, too. Do him good to get a little real exercise."

"But you should have the swimming pool in order at all times," Cara said earnestly. "I am sure the doctors told you — " she caught her breath as she realized she had said the hated word, but then went on — "to swim whenever you could, especially during the summer."

"I have Fred take me down to the Sound occasionally," Joshua Butler said. "But you're right. The pool is more convenient, and I'll tell Paul to go ahead and do a real job on it. Paul, you know, is going to inherit this estate."

"Yes, Brent said something about it," Cara acknowledged, uncertain how many details she was supposed to know.

"Paul always liked the place, and I'd thought he'd marry and settle down here. But now I don't know. Paul hasn't shown any interest in getting married, and Susan's husband has died and left her a mighty small life insurance. I've been thinking of selling the place so as to have a little more cash to spread around."

"But why do you tell me?" Cara asked. "Surely, whether you keep the estate or sell it or give it to Paul, I have no right to say anything at all about it."

"Oh, yes, you have!" Joshua Butler's gaze was sharp, but it was also fond. "Since I met you and found Brent had the good sense to plan to marry a girl with both feet on the ground, I've been wondering if I shouldn't reconsider the terms of my will. I've been thinking about it, anyway, for quite a spell. How would you like it, my dear — " he reached over and picked up Cara's left hand, turning it so that the diamonds sparkled in the soft glow of the candle-light — "if I gave this place to Brent now as an outright gift? Then you could fix the rose garden to suit yourself when he brings you here as a bride. Maybe you could even let an old man come and visit you for a while. It would be good to see the place looking its best again, and I'm selfish enough to enjoy having a pretty girl sit across from me at the dinner table. What do you say?" he finished.

Cara looked at him, aghast. What could she say? How could she tell Brent's kindly uncle that he was basing his future on a miserable fraud? It had never occurred to her it would make any difference to Uncle Josh if she played a false role for just a few weeks. How wrong she had been!

8

"GOOD day for sailing!" called Paul Rogers, looking over the hedge into the rose garden, where Cara was busy snipping dead leaves off bushes.

"It was," she returned, "but now it's nearly five . . . "

"Plenty of good sailing weather left," retorted Paul. "Hour, hour and a half, and you'll work up an appetite for dinner."

Cara laughed. "What I need is something that depresses the appetite. I've gained a pound since I've been at Soundings."

"On you it looks good." Paul grinned at her. "Want to join me? I need a crew. Have you ever tried being a one-man crew?"

"One summer when I was young, sixteen or so I had a vacation on the shore of a lake, and the people I was staying with had a sailboat. That is, the son of the house did; he was twenty. I crewed for him, but I'm afraid we both suffered."

She stopped, remembering those exciting hours spent dodging the swing of the boom above her head and otherwise risking a concussion, if not a fractured skull.

"I learned about sailing the hard way," she finished, laughing.

"One experienced crew," said Paul gravely. "Just what I need. Sign on?"

"Why not?" said Cara lightly. "As you say, it's great for sailing weather. An hour on the Sound! It's a temptation, and I'm falling for it."

"Bring a sweater or a foul weather jacket or something," Paul called after her as she started for the house. "You never know when there'll be a squall . . . "

Cara waved to show she had heard and dashed upstairs to change. She had a pair of dungarees — cut them off at the knees and they'd do fine. A pull-over and a sweater under her arm — oh, better tie her hair back. She found a red ribbon, tied her hair straight back from her face and observed the effect in the mirror. She looked young, she decided; more like the sixteen she had been when she had spent that summer sailing than the twenty-two she was now. Then she laughed at her reflection. She was taking a lot of pains with her appearance — as if that mattered to Paul!

Feeling like a culprit — for she was defying Brent — Cara went softly down the stairs. She did not intend to tell anyone where she was going.

Not that it's a secret. I'll tell Uncle Josh and Susan Evans all about it at dinner, when I get back, she assured herself. Brent? Well, Brent wasn't there, was he? He and Diane were probably spending the afternoon enjoying some kind of metropolitan fun; she had a right to a little harmless fling such as sailing on the Sound.

Brent had been gone since the day before yesterday. It had been courteous of him to drive Diane to New York, but did he have to stay so long? The hours had dragged, Cara admitted to herself, feeling a little foolish about it. She and Brent were not engaged and never would be. It was unreasonable of her to feel neglected or to resent his absence. All right, so she was unreasonable!

Paul was waiting by his car when she came out, wearing an old gray sweat shirt and faded sun-tans.

"I've phoned the marina; the *Sound Sprite* will be ready for us," he told her, opening the door for her. "It's not far to our port of call."

In less than half an hour they were heading into the wind, their boat dancing over the sunlit waves of the Sound, the sails filled. Cara, on the starboard side, sitting on the gunwale, looked at Paul, his face absorbed, alert, as she had never seen him.

"You like sailing, don't you?" she

asked, idly watching the green shore they had just left.

"Love it," said Paul.

"Does Brent go in for sailing, too?" Cara asked. Paul threw her a quizzical glance.

"He doesn't go in for sailing, golf, tennis or any sports," he answered. "Says he gets all the exercise and excitement he needs in his work. Did he ever tell you about his experience when he was lost for nearly a week in a tropical swamp? Getting out of tight spots like that is his idea of fun."

"It's my idea of horror," said Cara. "Alligators, snakes, quicksand — ugh!"

"I'm with you there," said Paul. "It's another thing on which we see eye to eye. Duck, Cara; the boom's headed your way!" He had jumped to his feet and was busy manipulating lines, trimming the mainsail. The boom swung above her, barely missing her, in fact, as she slid off her seat on the gunwale, scraping the skin off one side of her leg.

"Not much help, am I?" she said ruefully.

Nevertheless, now that she was faced with an emergency, the things she had learned about sailing that long ago summer came back to her. She found she knew what to do when Paul shouted to her to hoist the spinnaker or pull up the starboard line, and she shivered with excitement when he yelled, "Ready about!" and other nautical terms, responding automatically with the right performances.

"Are we going to sea?" she asked jokingly when she was able to relax once more, sitting on the gunwale. But Paul did not smile.

"We're not going anywhere for the time being," he said. "The wind's dying. Don't you see the sails?"

She glanced apprehensively in the direction Paul was gazing and saw the sails were slacking.

"But only a little while ago," she began, "the wind seemed to be singing in the sails . . . "

"Then isn't now," said Paul. "Now we are about to be becalmed."

"For how long?" Cara's face was worried as she looked toward the west. The sun had not yet set. Good!

"How should I know?" Paul sounded annoyed. "I'm not the weather forecaster." Then, at Cara's stricken expression, he sat near her and patted her hand. "Nothing to worry about," he assured her. "The wind is bound to return — sooner or later."

"Well, unless it's sooner, we're going to be late for dinner." Cara spoke matter-of-factly, but she was uneasy. She wished she had told someone in the household where she was going.

"We'll be lucky if we don't miss dinner," Paul told her.

"Will they worry, do you think?"

"Who? Sue Evans? Not she. We're both missing, remember. She'll simply point out we're off skylarking somewhere, probably foraging for our own food. Uncle Josh will be furious, of course."

"I feel very badly about that."

"At me, not you," said Paul. "He'll know it was my fault. Probably disinherit me within the hour."

Cara felt her cheeks, already reddened by the sun and wind, grow hotter still. Evidently Paul had no suspicion that her 'engagement' to Brent had threatened his inheritance. Nervously Cara asked:

"Is there anything we can do? Signal for help? The Coast Guard . . . "

Paul's answer to this startled her. He pulled her down to the cockpit, his arms tightened around her, and he kissed her till she gasped.

"Paul!" She finally struggled free and tried to get up, but he refused to let her rise.

"My dear little innocent, the Coast Guard's duties do not include getting becalmed sailors home to dinner. They have more important things to do. Now sit up here on the gunwale again and talk to me nicely." He helped her up, and she sat down on the gunwale again. She was silent for some minutes.

"Why the sphinx bit?" asked Paul lightly. "Do you want me to apologize for the kiss? Didn't you like it — a little bit?" His tone was so boyishly anxious that Cara laughed in spite of herself.

"You're very kissable, you know," Paul went on, "especially when you talk about calling the Coast Guard. Honest, sweetie, you sounded as if you meant it. And you looked about twelve years old, with the wind — the late wind — and the salt spray in your hair . . . "

Cara hastily put her hand to her hair. The red ribbon was gone, and her hair was plastered in wet ringlets against her forehead.

"What a sight I must be!" she exclaimed, forgetting she had meant to maintain a stony silence.

"There! The cat hasn't got your tongue after all," said Paul, in an exaggeratedly relieved tone. "Now that we're on speaking terms again, what shall we talk about?"

"You," said Cara imprudently. "That's

your favorite topic, isn't it?"

"How right you are, Carissima. But may I extend the scope of our conversation a little and talk about you and me?"

"I wish the wind would come up," said Cara.

"It will, it will, all in good time. But while we're here let's make the most of togetherness, shall we? Tell me, for instance, if you've finally and irrevocably decided to marry Brent, or if there's a chance for me?"

"Under the circumstances, that's not a fair question," Cara told him firmly. "I'm changing the subject right now. Tell me about your Uncle Joshua or Mrs. Evans."

"I will not!" cried Paul. "Two people in a romantic situation like this, and you want to talk about a couple of other people!"

"I feel a breeze," said Cara.

"By golly!" Paul looked up at the sails which were stirring slightly. "You're right! The wind has sprung up. 'Sailing,

sailing, over the bounding main,'" he sang, seizing the tiller.

"Oh, Paul, maybe we'll be in time for dinner after all!"

Paul took his eyes from the sails long enough to stare at her in feigned astonishment.

"I would have brought along a couple of hamburgers if I'd known I'd be likely to have a starving woman on my hands," he observed. "Well, here we go," as the sails filled. "Home is the sailor — practically — home from the sea . . . "

* * *

Lights along the shore and on other boats transformed the Sound of the afternoon into a mysterious region of purple and gold. There was no moon as yet, and the stars were just beginning to be visible as they reached the marina. It had been a silent return, after Paul's first effervescence as the wind came back, and Cara felt oddly despondent.

What a way to repay Uncle Joshua's kindness to her! As for Brent and his restrictions about seeing Paul . . .

I don't owe Brent Butler anything, Cara told herself. He hired me to do a job, and I've tried to do it, under very difficult circumstances. But it was a mistake to undertake this masquerade in the first place. It is living a lie, and no good can possibly come of it.

Now that she thought back on it, Cara wondered why she had agreed to the deception in the beginning. True, she had wanted to break the routine of her existence — the ordered life of the hospital, the unending round of sick beds, fretful patients, the often frustrating days when nothing she did seemed worthwhile.

I wish I'd never left it! she thought now, her eyes on the darkened sky. Why, I loved my life. I wonder why I thought I needed a change.

Her mind went back to her little apartment in Greenwich Village. It seemed adorably cosy in retrospect

— small, neat, compact; very different from her enormous room at Soundings, where nothing in the room belonged to her, except her clothes, and they were ordinary, unimaginative in comparison with the creations that enhanced Diane Forbes' beauty.

The thought of Diane brought up again the image of Brent Butler slipping under the wheel of Diane's car, and the sultry brunette glancing sideways in a practiced provocative look as the car swept down the drive.

"Cat's got your tongue again, I see," Paul commented dryly.

"I'm sorry, Paul. I just got to thinking about Diane Forbes. She's very beautiful, isn't she?"

Paul shrugged. "She'll get by," he said grudgingly. "But seriously," he added, "Diane's a frustrated female. She is bound and determined she's going to land Brent in her matrimonial net, and it will do him no good to keep up the struggle to get away. I don't know what she sees in the guy. But that's the way it is with her."

"Are you trying to tell me something, Paul?"

"I'm trying to tell you not to stub your toe on an insurmountable obstacle. Maybe you can beat Diane at her own game, but you should be warned. You may get hurt."

"It's a chance I'll have to take," Cara said, wondering what Paul's reaction would be if she were to tell him that, as far as she was concerned, Diane need not worry. Perhaps, she thought to herself, Brent had planned this curious engagement with the thought of making Diane jealous!

"I don't see why you say Diane is frustrated," Cara went on, watching the shore lights come closer and closer. "I gather she has enough money to indulge herself in any whim — even to pursuing a man halfway round the world, as she did Brent. She's the least inhibited person I have ever known."

"Nevertheless I stick to my original diagnosis," Paul said with a grin. "Just call me Dr. Rogers, noted psychiatrist. You were along the other night when she was driving us back from the races. That's not a normal way to drive. She was taking out her feelings of frustration on the wheel of the car."

"But she's a wonderful driver," Cara said, feeling she owed at least that much of a compliment to Diane.

"Sure she's wonderful — and lucky," Paul said grimly. "But she'd better learn to control herself or she'll get herself killed, along with anybody who happens to be riding with her. Well, here we are at the pier."

"Yes, here we are," echoed Cara, depressed at the thought of how late they were and how hurt and angry Uncle Josh was going to be. She would just have to take her medicine, and it didn't help any to realize she had done a very foolish and inconsiderate thing in accepting Paul's invitation to go sailing without saying anything to her host.

9

"CHIN up!" With a steadying hand under Cara's arm, Paul Rogers helped her out of the car. The house at Soundings was a blaze of light against the velvet softness of the sky. But it was quiet, very quiet. Cara shivered.

"Frankly, I'm scared," she admitted with a shaky laugh. "We not only don't get back in time for dinner; we get back way after dark. I think Mr. Joshua Butler is going to have me fired."

"Fired? What an odd thing to say, Cara."

"Just a figure of speech," she said hastily. She was saved from further explanation by the opening of the door.

Brent Butler, pressing the light over the entrance, stood looking at them with a lowering expression. Cara was aware that her dungarees were wrinkled and her pullover ripped; something had happened when she reached toward a sail. Paul Rogers did not look much better; he too was mud-stained and disheveled.

"I suppose you have an explanation for this escapade?" Brent said coldly.

"We went for a sail," Paul said airily, "and got becalmed. Of course we didn't know you were coming back tonight," he said pointedly.

"Did you have a good time in New York?" Cara asked.

"Don't change the subject," Brent snapped.

"If you two love birds will pardon me," Paul said with heavy sarcasm, "I'll go out in the kitchen and see if Mrs. Kelty can rustle me up a sandwich. I'm sure she would get one for you, too, Cara, if you have any appetite — after eating crow, that is." He vanished toward the kitchen.

"Get lost," said Brent briefly. He glanced toward the far end of the hall where Fred Bates was standing and added, "Tell Uncle Josh Cara is home and she is all right."

"I'm home, but I'm not all right," Cara contradicted, looking at him defiantly. "I've got a splitting headache, and if you can't think of anything pleasant to say, I'm going upstairs and take a shower."

"If what I say is unpleasant, it's because you are acting like an irresponsible child. I told you to stay away from Paul . . . "

"I know what you told me. Then you went off to New York with Diane Forbes."

"I thought I could trust you."

"Oh, for heaven's sake," Cara said in exasperation, "I'm getting tired of this whole mess. I'll pack up tomorrow and leave, and then you won't have to worry about me any more." Cara turned toward the stairs, surprised and annoyed to find her eyes were smarting. Then all at once she turned back. "You'd better take this." She held out the sapphire ring.

Brent shook his head.

"All right," said Cara, "if that's the way you want it. I'll leave it upstairs on the bureau. I'll have to borrow the convertible, if you don't mind; you can pick it up at the garage near my apartment."

"So you're running out on me. To you this was just another job — one you could throw over your shoulder any time you pleased."

"You were the one who said it was a job," Cara said wearily, "but I'm not going to stand here arguing all night."

"You don't care what happens to Uncle Josh, then?"

"I care very much indeed," Cara said angrily. "I have grown fond of your uncle, and I am happy to say he does not appear to be seriously ill. As a matter of fact, he is one of the reasons I think we'd better call this little thing off right now. Your uncle has offered to change his will and give you Soundings."

"I don't care about that."

Cara shrugged. "You can talk it over with him. I'm going back to New York. But if I may point out one flaw in your reasoning, it is this: if you are really worried about your uncle's health, you should get him to a doctor. I cannot give you a diagnosis. That's final."

Cara turned and stalked up to her room. She was angry enough so that she did not break down before the door had closed behind her. Then, as she punched the light button and looked around the large, luxurious room, she could no longer restrain the tears.

This is what comes of trying to be something I am not, she scolded herself. I have a good profession; I am a competent nurse. I should never have allowed myself to be talked into pretending I have anything in common with an empty-headed creature like Diane Forbes. If that is the type Brent wants, he's welcome to her. I'm never going to see him again.

* * *

Cara was up and packed and dressed by seven-thirty the next morning. It was not, she thought to herself wryly, the hour a debutante would arise. But she was through with pretending. She would go downstairs and ask Mrs. Kelty for a cup of coffee, then try to see Uncle Josh and thank him for his hospitality.

There was a light tap on the door, and Cara called, "Come in!" expecting for one unreasoning minute that perhaps Brent would not let her go after all. But it was Susan Evans who came in, her straight brown hair combed hastily back from her face and a green silk housecoat over her pajamas.

"I suspected you were going to get up at dawn and take off," Sue Evans said, settling herself on the bed and lighting a cigarette.

"Did Brent tell you I was leaving?"

"My dear, he didn't have to. I was in the living room last night, and while I couldn't hear what you said, I knew you were quarreling. Then when I talked to Brent afterward, he told me you'd broken the engagement."

"So there's nothing left for me to say but goodbye," Cara said, attempting to smile. "But you could do me one favor. Brent would not take his ring back, and I don't like to leave it lying here on the dresser. Would you give it to him for me, please?"

"I'm sorry I can't do that," Susan said positively. "I don't want to get involved. If you give the ring to anyone, I suggest you give it to my brother Josh. I presume you are going to say goodbye to him?"

"Of course I'm going to say goodbye!" Cara said, hurt at Susan's tone. "He has been very kind, and I have enjoyed my stay here. Please say goodbye to Linda for me. You know, I'm sure, she's compounding a White Magic powder which is supposed to make your brother completely well."

"I'll say goodbye to Linda," Susan

promised. "But I do think you should see Brent again. He may have quarreled with you last night, but after all, he had great provocation. When he came back from New York, you and Paul were missing, and no one had any idea where you'd gone. My brother finally thought to call up the marina, and that was when he discovered you had taken the sailboat."

"Brent has a strange way of showing he was worried," Cara commented. "Anyway, Susan, I think what has happened between Brent and me is hardly your affair."

"I expected you to tell me it was none of my business," Susan said imperturbably, "but you're wrong. You see, I was the person who talked with Diane Forbes. I was the one who told her Brent was engaged. I was the one who invited her here. Believe me, my motives were of the best. I have heartily disliked Diane for years, and I was very happy when my favorite nephew got himself engaged to somebody else. So you see I'm responsible for your quarrel with Brent. If Diane hadn't been here, you would never have gone sailing with Paul, and there would have been no misunderstanding."

"It doesn't matter," Cara said dully.

Susan Evans didn't know — and of course Cara could not tell her — that there had been no actual engagement; that she was a nurse, and the masquerade party was now over.

There was a slight noise at the door, and as Cara and Susan turned they saw Linda standing there in crumpled yellow pajamas, her eyes looking bigger and shinier than ever, her straight black hair obviously uncombed. Cara was sorry she had not had a chance to see the child and tell her she was going away. The little girl appeared to be rigid with shock.

"You were going away without telling me," she said accusingly. "Why do you have to go away?"

"Now, Linda," Susan said briskly, "remember your manners. I've told you not to question grown-ups about where they go or what they do. It isn't polite."

But Cara thought the small figure looked inexpressibly forlorn. She crossed the room swiftly and took both thin elbows in her hands.

"I wouldn't have gone away without saying goodbye, Linda. I've grown very fond of you, and I'm greatly interested in our secret formula. Of course I won't be here when you get it finished, but I think if you tell Unc' Josh about it, he will understand just as I did."

But Linda had an unchildlike way of sticking to the main point. "Are you going away because of that lady who was here a couple of days ago?"

Cara glanced at Susan in alarm. The child must have overheard her mother's comments on Diane Forbes.

"You're too young to understand," Linda's mother said. "Run along and get dressed, and maybe Cara will let you walk out to the car with her."

It was the wrong way to handle

Linda, Cara thought as the little girl looked mutinous. But of course her mother had her own methods, and the nurse could not contradict them. She tried to say with reasonable conviction:

"Diane had nothing to do with it, Linda. Please believe me."

"She did too," said Linda. "She sang bad songs."

"You were listening!" her mother accused her. "You know that's naughty, Linda."

"But she sang in French!" Cara exclaimed.

"Linda understands French," Linda's mother said, looking rather upset. Cara remembered Uncle Josh's comment that it was just as well she did not know the language, and she gathered Diane's French songs had been too spicy for a child's ears.

"She's a bad lady," Linda declared with conviction. "She made you go away. She's bad, bad, bad." A sudden thought seemed to strike her, and she asked eagerly: "If I fix her so she can't come here, would you come back, Cara?"

"I've had enough of this," Linda's mother said in a voice of authority. She walked over to the door and took Linda's hand firmly in hers. Cara gave her a fleeting kiss on each cheek and smiled.

"Goodbye, Cara," Susan said, leading the child away. "I'm sure my brother will want you to come back to Soundings at least for the Fourth of July celebration. Come along, Linda."

Reluctantly Linda allowed herself to be pulled along the corridor. But she turned her elfin face and looked at Cara with a conspiratorial stare just before she went into her room. It was a look that boded no good for Diane Forbes, and Cara shivered as she considered what malevolent thoughts the child might have. Then she shrugged. Time was running out, and she had to see Joshua Butler before she left.

Joshua was already dressed and in his wheel chair when Cara went to his suite on the first floor. He did not seem surprised to see her, but instead told her to pull up a chair and sent for Bates to get fresh coffee.

"I have three things to do," Cara said, looking at him fondly. "I have to apologize for missing dinner last night; I have to thank you for your truly wonderful hospitality, and I have to say goodbye, because I'm going back to New York."

Joshua Butler took the coffeepot Bates had brought in and carefully poured her a cup of the steaming liquid. Then he handed the cup to her with a flash of amusement in his eyes.

"You didn't have to tell me. I may be chained to this wheel chair, but I have a good idea what goes on, and I know a girl of your spirit wouldn't accept the way my nephew has been acting. But you make it very hard on an old man, my dear, when you walk out of this house. I was looking forward to seeing that rose garden become a bower of beauty as it used to be. In fact, I am not going to let you go unless you promise you'll come back for our Fourth of July celebration."

"We'll see," Cara murmured, sipping her coffee.

"You can't expect the course of true love to run smooth," Joshua Butler said. "Just remember, after you've taught Brent his lesson, there's a place here waiting for you and an old man who will welcome you with open arms."

"You're a darling," Cara said, her eyes suspiciously moist. "But there's one thing I want to tell you before I go. Linda is convinced she can make up a powder and invoke the spirits of White Magic to make you all well again. I've made her promise she would show me the powder before she gave it to you. But if I'm not going to be here, I want you to watch out for it."

Uncle Josh threw back his head and laughed heartily. "I had an idea the little imp was up to something." He chuckled. "Have you any notion what will be in this powder?"

"I don't know all the ingredients," Cara admitted. "So far, I believe it will be properly dried and powdered dead beetles, chicken feathers, burned and also powdered, and I suppose a few weeds — whatever Linda can find around the place. I don't know how she expects to give it to you, but I think you should be careful when you take a glass of milk or any liquid in which this powder might be dissolved."

"If Linda has to burn those chicken feathers," Joshua observed, "I'll have ample warning that the powder is being prepared. There's no worse smell on earth than that of burning feathers."

"I'm sure Linda will forget about voodoo after she has lived away from Haiti for a few years," Cara said seriously. "And of course her White Magic is fairly amusing. But I don't like to think of Linda — or any child — trying to use Black Magic."

"My sister Susan seems to think all children go through a phase of believing in some kind of magic, whether it's white or black," Uncle Joshua remarked. "And I suppose she's right. I never had any children of my own. At any rate, when a child is nine years old 'the world is so full of a number of things.' She jumps from one absorbing subject to another so fast an oldster like me cannot keep up with her. I don't worry about Linda. Susan has a good practical head on her shoulders, and Linda's father was a sensible man, too, although he did not provide very well for the future of his family. The child has a good inheritance."

Cara did not see how she could press the point any further.

10

CARA was unprepared for the sight of her own apartment, which had seemed, from the cool reaches of Long Island, to be cosy and attractive. Instead, when she opened the door, she was met by a blast of hot, stale and musty-smelling air. Although she walked over to one of the two windows and opened it wide, it did not help much. Also, it seemed the place had become incredibly dusty; it would need a good morning's work to make it livable again.

There was no use standing around feeling sorry for herself, Cara thought, going into the tiny bedroom and struggling to open a window which was difficult either winter or summer. She found an old faded house-dress, tied a bandana around her hair and settled down to the serious business of scrubbing the apartment.

She had a vague hope that her housewifely activity would keep her from thinking about her last brief talk with Brent. She had found him waiting for her on the terrace after she had left Joshua's suite, and he had said remarkably little. He did say he was sorry she was going and he thought she ought to think it over for a while before making up her mind definitely. Cara had agreed with him because it seemed the simplest thing to do.

Brent had insisted she accept a check for five hundred dollars as payment for her 'work' at Soundings, and she had insisted he accept the sapphire ring and put it in a safe place.

"There's a garage about five blocks away from my apartment," she told him. "But I can't for the life of me remember the name of it, and of course they may not have room for the convertible, even for a few days."

"Don't worry about it," Brent said. "It's supposed to be your car, remember;

I can't very well bring it out here and announce that I bought it from you. Anyway, as long as you keep it, I'll always feel you might come back here."

But Cara still didn't like the thought of keeping anything as valuable as a convertible in the small and crowded garage where it was at the moment. She decided she would write to Brent and tell him where the car was. He could come in and pick up the keys or, if he did not want to do that, she would mail them back.

At the thought of Brent coming to the apartment, Cara started to work in earnest. Yet, as she had suspected, it took several hours before she felt the apartment was clean once more. She was too exhausted to prepare anything to eat, so she decided to have dinner at La Gondola Restaurant, a small Italian place around the corner.

When she reached the restaurant door, however, she was confronted with a neat placard announcing the proprietor had gone away on vacation. The restaurant would be open for business again on August first.

Cara toyed briefly with the idea of going to a smart and air-conditioned spot uptown, but it seemed too much effort. She finally bought herself a hamburger in a nearby drugstore and then went to a movie where it was at least cool. Soundings and the luxury living which she had known for the past few weeks were far, far away.

* * *

The next three days were three of the longest days Cara had ever known. When she was in the apartment the phone did not ring. When she went out she was sure that it rang again and again. She knew she ought to call the hospital and inquire about getting her old job back. Once she even went so far as to dial the number, only to hang up before it could be answered.

But bad as the days were, the nights

were even worse. She tried to tell herself she was being silly; Brent probably considered the incident finished, and Uncle Josh had no doubt forgotten his invitation to attend the Fourth of July celebration at the country club.

On the morning of the fourth day Cara got up and dressed carefully. She had given herself a good talking too the night before and had made her plans. She would not phone the hospital; she would go there and talk with the head nurse. The minute she said she was available, she knew she would be committed to go back to work. They were always short-handed in the summertime, when so many of the nurses took their vacations.

She was almost ready to go out of the door when the phone rang. But when she answered she had so steeled herself to forget about Soundings she was surprised to hear Brent's voice.

"Miss me?" he asked eagerly.

Cara managed a laugh which she hoped sounded amused. "I missed you madly! How are Uncle Josh and Susan and Linda?"

"They all miss you." Brent's voice sounded as if he really meant it. But then, remembering the last three lonely days, Cara forced herself to say:

"Tell them I was asking for them. When are you coming to town to pick up the car?"

"That's why I called. I have been named a committee of one to come in and get you and bring you back here. Seems you promised Uncle Josh you would be here for the Fourth of July, and you also had some secret project going with Linda. Paul is sulking because the swimming pool is all cleaned up and somewhat repaired and you're not here to tell him what a good job he did."

"You make me sound like the indispensable woman." Cara laughed. It probably wasn't true at all, but it was sweet to hear Brent say she had been missed.

"Enough of this chitchat," Brent said

briskly. I can catch a train immediately if not sooner. Will you put a few things in your travelling bag and be ready to come back with me when I get there?"

"I was just going to keep an appointment," Cara said, hoping to preserve a little of her pride. There was no doubt about it in her own mind: she really wanted to go back to the brooding brown house overlooking the Sound.

"Cancel your appointment," Brent said tersely. "I'm sure Uncle Josh feels he has priority."

"I'll be ready," Cara promised.

The past three days have not been entirely wasted, Cara told herself as she hastily took off the serviceable plaid cotton frock she had been going to wear to the hospital and instead put on her cream-colored cotton brocade which she had bought the day before. It made her pale hair look like moonlight, and it seemed to put a new sparkle into her eyes. She would not admit, even to herself, that the prospect of staying at Soundings for another week, and this time under her true colors, was responsible for making her eyes so bright.

She had decided, during her lonely hours in the apartment, that if she were invited back to Soundings she would insist upon telling Uncle Josh she was a registered nurse. If, when Brent told him the news, Joshua Brent felt he did not want to offer hospitality to one of her profession, she would simply come back to New York. But she would not again try to pretend she was a debutante or that she was Brent's fiancée.

It was unexpectedly difficult to give Brent an ultimatum when he came bounding up the stairs and into the apartment with a look of such eager joy all of Cara's good resolutions almost melted.

He did not attempt to kiss her, but instead put both hands on her shoulders and held her close for a minute. "You're even more beautiful than I remembered," he said huskily.

"And you're more handsome," answered Cara, keeping her voice steady with an effort. "Now that we've exchanged the usual compliments, come over and sit down here for a minute while I talk to you."

Brent dropped his hands immediately. "I remember," he said in a subdued voice. "No love-making except in public."

"And no love-making in public, either," Cara told him. "We broke our engagement, Brent, and that's the way it's going to be. I'll come out to Soundings, and I'd like to stay for the Fourth of July celebration. But only as a guest of Uncle Josh; not as your fiancée."

"Was it so hard to take? The fiancée bit, I mean?"

"Not hard at all, but I don't like to pretend, especially to someone I like and respect as much as I do your uncle."

"Couldn't we go on as we were?" Brent asked.

"I'm sorry, but the answer is no, definitely no. I also want you to tell your uncle I am a registered nurse."

"You know he doesn't like doctors and nurses."

"Then it is all the more important I not try to deceive him."

"But how will I explain why I invited you out to Soundings in the first place?"

"You invited me out as your fiancée," Cara reminded him. "Knowing how your uncle felt about the nursing profession, we did not tell him I was a nurse. But now that we are no longer engaged, there is no reason he should not know the truth. If your uncle doesn't want me to stay when you tell him about me, of course I will come back to New York at once."

"You sure make it hard for a guy," Brent complained. "But I suppose you have a right to lay down the rules this time — as I did a month ago. I don't worry about Uncle Josh tossing you out. Nurse or not, you are his favorite person, and I'm sure he'll be delighted to see you. By the way, we'd better get going. Where's your suitcase?"

"In the bedroom. I'll get it," Cara said, feeling as if a great weight had been lifted from her shoulders.

"I'm going to be awfully glad to see everyone again," she admitted, "especially Linda . . . "

"That's why we have to hurry. Linda met with a slight accident."

Cara stopped as if she had run into a stone wall, and slowly turned around. At her look of distress, Brent said hastily:

"Oh, it's nothing to worry about. My little cousin decided to ride her bike around the rim of the swimming pool. Paul repaired it, you know, but there were a few bumps. Linda hit one and apparently flew over the handle bars and landed on her head on the concrete."

"Did she fall into the pool?"

"No, she landed on the concrete apron, luckily. She was knocked out for a while; we don't know how long. Paul found her and brought her back to the house. Mrs. Kelty put her to bed, but she came to almost at once and wanted to get up."

"I suppose Susan has taken her to the hospital by now," Cara said, feeling much relieved.

"Susan isn't there today. A friend of hers is getting married in a garden ceremony with all the trimmings somewhere up in Maine. The kid's all right, I tell you. She was a little sick to her stomach before I came out, but Mrs. Kelty can take care of that . . . "

"Mrs. Kelty indeed!" Cara exclaimed angrily. "Linda probably has a concussion and is running a fever. Close the windows for me while I pack my uniforms. We've got to get to Soundings and get there fast."

* * *

Cara knew Brent drove the convertible to the very limit of the law, but the drive out to the house seemed terribly long. She kept telling herself that with Mrs. Kelty to keep the child quiet and in bed, no serious harm could come to her for the time being. Nevertheless, when they turned into the neglected driveway and drew up in front of the terrace, Cara was out of the car as soon as it stopped. She ran up to Linda's room and met Mrs. Kelty just coming out the door. The heavy-seat, middle-aged woman looked worried.

"That's the third time she's vomited since we put her to bed," the woman said without preamble. "I don't like it, Miss Cara. I think I'll go down and talk to Mr. Butler myself. I want the child to see a doctor."

Cara looked in; Linda was lying back on the pillow, looking shrunken and very white. Her eyes were closed.

"I'm not going to wait for Uncle Josh to change his mind and send for a doctor, Mrs. Kelty," she said, and the woman recognized the ring of authority in her voice. "I'll wrap her up and take her down to the car. There's a very good hospital at Glen Rock, and it's only a few minutes away. We'll get her there and have them do an X-ray. You can tell Mr. Butler about it afterward. I'll take the blame."

Brent had followed her upstairs and seemed to understand what she meant to do without explanation. He scooped up the child, blanket and all, in his arms and said when she opened her eyes:

"Cara's back. The first thing she's going to do is take you for a ride."

"Hi, Linda!" Cara said with a casual air, not wanting to alarm the child, "I hear you fell off your bike."

"I hurt my head," Linda explained, her big eyes looking cloudy and dull. "I wish Mimbo was here. He'd make the pain go away."

"I know a place where they have some White Magic," Cara said quickly. "It's a little different from Mimbo's kind, but it works pretty well anyway. They'll take away your headache."

"Will they stop me being sick, too?" asked Linda, her voice already weaker.

"They can do anything," Cara assured her, sliding behind the wheel of the car. Brent, with the now unconscious Linda in his arms, got into the seat beside her, and Cara whipped the car around and went back down the drive.

They spent almost two hours at the hospital. Cara immediately liked young Dr. Crane, who kept Linda amused while he took the X-rays by pretending she was a beauty queen and they needed pictures of her from every angle to put in the newspapers. Linda obediently held the pose time after time.

After the X-rays had been taken, Cara went with a nurse up to the children's wing and helped put Linda to bed. The child was exceedingly drowsy, and when she tried to keep her eyes open and make conversation the effort was obvious. Cara assured her repeatedly that she would not leave, and finally Linda, holding tightly to her hand, fell into an uneasy sleep.

Downstairs, later, Dr. Crane confirmed the fact that Linda had a slight concussion, undoubtedly sustained when she hit her head on the concrete after she fell from her bicycle. Because she had been several hours without proper care, the condition had been aggravated and she was running a fever.

"You'll have to leave her here overnight, of course," Dr. Crane said with a smile. "It might be better if she stayed here a couple of days. But you needn't worry about her, Miss Merrill. Mr. Butler told me while you were upstairs that you are a nurse, so I don't have to tell you how quickly children of Linda's age, who are basically strong and healthy, can recover."

"Yes, I'm sure she'll be all right, now that she's in your hands," Cara said. "But I dread telling Joshua Butler that his favorite and only niece is going to be hospitalized."

Dr. Crane grinned at her sympathetically. "I've heard what Joshua Butler thinks about hospitals and doctors," he said. "I don't envy you having to break the news."

11

JOSHUA BUTLER was waiting for them on the terrace when Cara and Brent returned to Soundings. He did not look so fierce to Cara as she came toward him. Instead she felt a pang of pity for the man sitting in the wheel chair; he seemed somehow to have shrunk, in spite of his broad shoulders and leonine head. His bushy eyebrows were drawn together, but he said nothing, and it was Brent who broke the difficult silence.

"We've taken Linda to the hospital, sir. I'm sorry there wasn't time to ask you about it before we left."

"It's a concussion, Uncle Josh," Cara said gently. "Linda will have to stay in the hospital for a few days until they reduce her fever."

Joshua Butler still said nothing but continued to eye the two of them coldly.

"If you think we did wrong, sir — " Brent began at last, but his uncle interrupted harshly:

"What kind of monster do you think I am? Of course if Linda needs hospital care, she should have it. I don't want anything to happen to that child. Nobody told me she was so sick."

"A good many children fall off their bikes," Cara said, trying to make it easier for the worried old man. "Often they are not hurt at all. But when, as in Linda's case, a child hits her head, there is always the possibility of concussion."

"How about saying hello to your host in the proper manner?" Uncle Josh barked at Cara.

"I don't dare," Cara said, with a meaningful glance at Brent. "I told your nephew that he would have to tell you the truth about me; when you hear it you may not want me to stay for the Fourth of July celebration."

Thus prompted, Brent began slowly to explain that Cara was a registered nurse, but that because of Uncle Josh's known aversion to nurses and doctors in general they had been afraid to tell him the truth. However, Brent added, and Cara was surprised at his hurt tone, Cara had definitely refused to accept Uncle Josh's hospitality a second time unless he knew the facts.

"Quite right, too," Joshua Butler said sharply. "I don't like people who sail under false colors. But I hope you're going to stay with us for a while. We have all missed you, and we need not refer to your unfortunate choice of profession. You're here not as a nurse but as a guest."

"You're a darling!" Cara said. She bent swiftly and kissed him happily on both cheeks. Joshua Butler's embrace was hearty, and he was smiling broadly when he finally let her go.

"Now that's all settled," he said with a chuckle. "I suppose I'd better go back to my room and get out the engagement ring again. Or you can do it for me, Brent . . . Brent asked me to keep it for him," he said to Cara.

"Well, you see, Uncle Josh," Brent said hesitantly, "Cara doesn't want to be engaged to me any more. So you'd better just hang onto the ring."

"What's the matter with my nephew?" Joshua Butler demanded. "Any engaged couple has a lovers' quarrel now and then. But that's no reason to break off the engagement for good and all."

"I just am not sure Brent and I are really suited to each other," Cara said haltingly. "We did get engaged rather quickly," she went on, with a sidelong glance at Brent. "We should have thought it over carefully before we took such an important step."

"Fiddle-faddle, as Mrs. Kelty would say," Uncle Josh said testily. "If two people are in love, there's no use to discuss the pros and cons of the future like a Philadelphia lawyer. Now you listen to me, Brent," he said forcefully. "You're my favorite nephew, but I'm very disappointed in you. You found one girl in a million, and now you're about to let her slip through your fingers."

"I'll try to patch things up, Uncle Josh," Brent promised, looking at Cara with narrowed eyes. She felt faintly uneasy; Brent looked as if he meant it! She started to protest, but Joshua Butler cut her short.

"See that you do patch things up," he said testily to Brent. "That's an order."

* * *

Susan Evans left the house party in Maine as soon as she heard Linda was in the hospital. She went directly to see her child and stayed with her most of the day. Cara had thought she herself might go over to the hospital, but when she heard Linda's mother was there she decided against it.

It was pleasant to be back at Soundings once more. Paul had accepted her return with delight and apparently had been told her engagement to

Brent was off. He found occasion to whisper to Cara under cover of the hum of conversation at the dinner table that he was glad to know he had a chance to put forward his own claims as a suitor.

"You've got to give me equal time, at least, as they say on the TV networks," Paul insisted.

"Oh, you're talking about candidates who have been nominated to run for office," Cara teased. "Who nominated you as a candidate, Paul?"

"I nominated myself," he said laughing with her but with an undercurrent of seriousness in his manner. "I want a chance to prove I have many sterling qualities. I am young, healthy, interested in sports, and could qualify for a job as maintenance man on any estate in the country. Wait till you see how I've fixed up the swimming pool! Also, my prospects are good," he added in a lower tone.

Before Cara had a chance to answer him, Joshua Butler inquired of Paul if he had been able to reach Susan. Paul assured him that he had and that Linda was doing fine. After that the conversation became general.

The next morning Uncle Josh called Cara to his suite right after breakfast. After some beating about the bush, he told her he had decided not to tell Paul or his half-sister Susan that she was a nurse. Cara was surprised, but she agreed at once to Joshua Butler's dictum. It did not seem to her it made much difference whether or not Susan and Paul knew she was a nurse.

Later on, when she was talking to Brent, she found he had a ready explanation.

"My Uncle Josh is afraid of losing face," he told Cara with a grin. "After the way he's ranted and raved against both doctors and nurses, he doesn't dare admit *you've* been able to make him let down the bars. But then of course he never met anyone like you — and I never have either. How about taking the ring back, Cara?"

"I couldn't do that, Brent," Cara said, shaking her head. "It wouldn't be honest."

"No girl I know would split hairs the way you do," Brent said impatiently. "At least you might try being engaged. For real, I mean."

"Have you ever been engaged before, Brent?"

"Positively never."

"Not even to Diane Forbes?"

"No." Brent was positive, but he looked uncomfortable. "When I was going to college I used to run around with her. We were in the same crowd, and we went to dances and on skiing jaunts in the Laurentians — that sort of thing. But she knew there was never anything serious between us."

"I wonder," Cara mused, as much to herself as to Brent, "if you are really ready, even yet, to be serious about anyone. You want me to wear your grandmother's beautiful ring almost on a trial basis . . . "

"I didn't mean that at all," Brent protested. "I was only hoping, if you wore the ring, you might get into the habit of being engaged to me. But never mind," he added. "We'll talk about this another time."

That afternoon Paul insisted they have a proper christening party for the newly renovated pool. Uncle Josh was agreeable, and when Fred Bates brought him down in his wheel chair he was already in bathing trunks. And as Cara had expected, once he was in the water Uncle Josh was again a whole man. He was a strong swimmer, and there was no hint of his infirmity as he tossed the water ball first to Brent and then to Paul with forceful aim. He soon had both his nephews working hard to return his volleys.

Cara sat on the rim of the pool, cheering Uncle Josh and making derogatory comments when Brent or Paul fumbled. She felt again as she often had during her training program and later when she was called upon to take care of a polio patient. What a terrible waste it was for a man like Uncle Josh to be so crippled! How could he downgrade the medical profession?

Somehow, she thought to herself, I must convince Joshua Butler that continuing research is the only way we can ever feel reasonably safe from polio or anything else that strikes a man down in the prime of life or condemns children to a lifetime of pain and suffering. If only the Salk vaccine had been discovered earlier, maybe Uncle Josh . . .

Paul had indeed done a nice job renovating the pool. The rim was comparatively smooth, and Paul had painted it a bright blue. The water was clear and cold, and they all enjoyed relaxing and kidding each other. Kelty arrived with a tray of canapés and a bottle of champagne.

"Champagne?" Brent asked, raising his eyebrows.

"You can't have a christening party

without a bottle of champagne," Paul said with dignity. "Thanks, Uncle Josh, for raiding your cellar. I see Kelty has it chilled. Wait a minute, and I'll perform the proper ceremony."

"You're not going to break the bottle on the rim of the pool!" Cara exclaimed in horror.

"Certainly not," laughed Uncle Josh. "This is going to be a different kind of christening. We'll consider the popping of the cork a substitute for breaking the bottle, and then we'll all drink a toast to my nephew Paul."

"Am I in time to join the party?" asked Susan Evans gaily. She came toward them along the path, still dressed in a lightweight suit in a particularly becoming shade of rose. She looked happy and relaxed.

To their queries about Linda, she said thankfully the child was doing all right; she had responded beautifully to medication. She would be able to bring her child home the next day, Susan reported, although the doctor advised that Linda be kept reasonably quiet and avoid all strenuous exercise for the time being.

"I understand I have you to thank, Cara, for getting Linda to the hospital so promptly," Susan said gratefully.

"I would have seen to it Linda had proper care," Uncle Josh protested.

"Of course, Uncle Josh," Cara said diplomatically. "Sometimes in mild cases of concussion, a child is dizzy only for an hour or two, and then recovers completely."

Paul and Susan were looking at her curiously and Brent threw her a warning glance. Cara could have bitten off her tongue. What had possessed her to sound off on the subject of concussion?

"Well, we're going to have our little imp back again tomorrow," Uncle Josh said hastily. "But today, Susan, we are christening our refurbished swimming pool. Will you join us in a glass of champagne?"

"She can share mine," Cara said,

"and then Kelty won't have to go back for another glass. Since we are launching the swimming pool, so to speak, shouldn't we give it a name?"

"Let's call it Dunker's Delight," said Paul brightly.

"You make it sound like a cup of coffee," objected Brent. "I'd prefer something more whimsical, such as Do Drop In."

Paul groaned. "How whimsical can you get?" he demanded.

"I think we'd better forget the naming ceremony," Uncle Josh said. Fred Bates had helped him out of the pool, and he was wrapped in a bathrobe with a light blanket over his knees, but Cara saw he was beginning to look chilled. "Let's drink a toast to Paul and consider the ceremony completed. I'll have to get up to the house and get dressed."

"To our very clever relative, Paul Rogers," Susan said, taking a sip of champagne and passing the glass to Cara. Everyone obediently raised his glass toward Paul and drank. Then, Cara, before passing her glass back to Susan, had a sudden inspiration.

"To Joshua Butler," she said happily, "Susan's brother, Paul and Brent's uncle and my very dear — my very, very dear — and incomparable host!"

Cara had intended it as just a laughing tribute to Joshua Butler, but she was surprised, when she looked toward him, to see that his eyes were moist and suspiciously bright.

After Uncle Josh had gone, the four of them sat around the pool, chattering aimlessly. Susan told them about the wedding she had almost attended. She had had the best part of the festivities anyway, she added hastily, before she was called back by the news of Linda's accident.

There had been a farewell party for the bride which the groom-to-be and other male members of the wedding group had crashed successfully. That night there had been a bachelor's dinner for the groom, and the bridesmaids had turned the tables and insisted upon joining in.

"It sounds so gay," Cara said wistfully. "Is the bride very beautiful?"

"She reminded me of you," Susan said with a smile. "She has the same pale gold hair. But her eyes are blue, and I don't think she's quite as tall as you are. She told me confidentially they're going to honeymoon out at a ranch her father owns in Colorado. She's a very down-to-earth person, and Jimmy, the boy she's marrying, is a nice guy."

"Was Diane Forbes among those present at the festivities?" Paul asked casually. It seemed to Cara that Brent stiffened slightly at mention of the brunette's name.

"She was supposed to be a bridesmaid," Susan said, "but she had to call it off because her father's coming over from Europe, and she wants to stay in New York and meet him. Don't I remember," she added, glancing at Brent, "that my brother invited her and her father to be with us for the Fourth of July at the country club celebration?"

Brent's expression was carefully deadpan. "I believe he did say something about it," he said indifferently.

"Seems funny to me," Paul commented, "that Diane would pass up a chance for such wedding hi-jinks just to drive her Dad out here to Soundings. Apparently she is dead serious about her visit here and won't allow herself to be diverted even by a gala party. Brent, my boy, you'd better watch yourself. From where I sit, you're the target."

Brent looked at him for a few seconds as he stood at the edge of the pool, holding his empty champagne glass aloft and grinning impudently. Suddenly, so quickly Paul did not have time to retreat, Brent rose and pushed Paul backward into the pool. Then he reached down and took Cara's hand and, without saying anything more, marched her off at a fast pace back to the house.

12

WHEN Susan Evans brought her daughter home, Linda was as full of bounce as ever, Paul observed. Linda evidently felt she had been on a great adventure. She ran up to her room, out to the terrace, and down to the swimming pool and back as if she had been away for a long, long time and couldn't wait to see the dear familiar surroundings.

Susan came rushing up to Cara's room just as she finished putting on her 'gardening' costume, which consisted of a pair of faded shorts and a plaid cotton poncho.

"I can't seem to control that child of mine," Susan said with exasperation. "She's supposed to keep quiet, but short of tying her to a chair I don't know how I'm going to manage. Could you help me out, Cara?"

"I'll try," Cara said cheerfully, "but of course Linda is pretty excited about having been in a hospital. Maybe if I let her tell me all about it she will calm down."

"But you probably want to spend some time alone with Brent," Susan said hesitantly.

"No, we've decided to stay unengaged," Cara explained with a smile. "Anyway, Paul and Brent are closeted with your brother, and I wouldn't want to disturb what is probably an important business meeting."

Whether Linda had worked off her first natural exuberance at being home and was genuinely tired, or whether she really welcomed the chance of talking with Cara alone, was hard to determine. At any rate, she went willingly with Cara to the rose garden and sat quietly on a bench, watching, while Cara weeded around the bushes and loosened the soil.

"It was a nice hospital you were in," Cara said, to break the conversational ice. "I like Dr. Crane, and I bet he liked you."

Linda nodded solemnly, her elfin face unsmiling and her big eyes looking even more enormous than usual.

"Dr. Crane uses White Magic, too," Linda said confidently. "I think maybe he could use it on Unc' Josh. But when I asked my uncle about it this morning, he got awful mad. Why does he get so mad, Cara? Don't he want to get well?"

"Of course he wants to get well," Cara said, "but he has a very complicated illness, Linda. It would be hard for you to understand."

"I don't have to understand it," Linda said with conviction. "I'm going to make up a powder like Mimbo used to do, and when Unc' Josh takes it he'll get all better."

Cara's first impulse was to protest this emphasis on a primitive ritual, and then she thought better of it. She was not going to change Linda's mind overnight; time and the new environment would soon make her forget. In the meantime, perhaps the preparation of the powder could be stretched a few days and would keep the child fairly quiet.

"Can you remember what it was Mimbo put in the powder besides dried lizard and bird and chicken feathers?" Cara asked. "Were there many ingredients?"

"Quite a lot," Linda said gravely. "It's funny, but when I was in the hospital they put a needle in my arm and I went right to sleep and dreamed for the longest time."

"Did the needle hurt?" Cara asked.

"No, not much." Evidently Linda's mind was on something more important. "Don't you want to know what I dreamed about?"

"Of course I do."

"I dreamed I was back home — in Haiti, I mean," Linda said softly. "It was night time, because the sky was all black. The stars were big and right almost on top of my head, like they used to be back home on the plantation. The stars here are little stars, Cara, and they're awful far away. But back home they're very big and so close you can reach up and touch them almost."

"Haiti must be a beautiful place," Cara agreed.

"I was home again," the child went on, and her eyes had a mystic look that made Cara shiver. "Mimbo was there, and he was smiling all over like he often did. I told him I wanted to make the White Powder Magic, and he told me just what to put in it."

"But you may not be able to get some of the ingredients," Cara pointed out. "You know we can't find any real lizards around here, and you were going to use the dried beetles instead."

"I told Mimbo that, and he said it was all right. I just went upstairs, and they're all nice and dry. I've got them in a jar on my window sill," Linda went on, "but I'll have to wait until the moon rises before I pound them until they're all powder."

The burned chicken feathers would present no problem, Linda explained further, because Mrs. Kelty had already promised to speak to the butcher and see that their next chicken was delivered with a few feathers thrown in. Another ingredient that was needed was a thimble full of pigeon's blood. Cara was about to protest when she suddenly remembered that soy sauce, a dark red liquid used in Chinese cooking, was probably available on Mrs. Kelty's pantry shelf.

Once she had promised to assist in assembling the ingredients, Linda was delighted to list them all. She should have green sugar cane, she explained to Cara, but finally agreed that green sugar would be close enough. There also had to be a plant which the child could not describe too closely and which Cara could not identify. However, it was purple in color, and Cara decided she could produce a reasonable facsimile of purple sap by the judicious use of food colouring.

"When you get this made up," Cara asked finally, "will it be a powder or a paste?"

"It will be a paste," Linda assured her. "You need a coconut shell full of rum. Can we get a coconut shell?" she inquired anxiously.

"I'll make sure you have a coconut shell," Cara promised. "Brent and I will travel the length and breadth of Long Island until we find just the perfect coconut shell to hold the rum and your magic powder. But if I help you, Linda, you must promise to do something for me in return. You must promise to stay quiet today and tomorrow."

"Why?" Linda demanded.

"Because you had some White Magic, too, and you have to give it time to work. Anyway," Cara said, with what she thought was inspiration, "you want to be completely well on the Fourth of July. We're all going over to the country club. Your Uncle Josh tells me they have beautiful fireworks about nine o'clock."

"Are we all going over?" Linda asked. "Mommy and Cousin Paul and Cousin Brent and you and Unc' Josh and everybody?"

"Yes, we'll all be there," Cara agreed. "Have you ever seen fireworks, Linda?"

"Oh, yes," said the child. "Back home we always had fireworks at Christmas. I'm glad you came back to stay with us," she added shyly. "You're nice, Cara. When you get married and live happily ever after, will you live here?"

"Don't rush me," Cara laughed, getting to her feet and brushing the dirt from her knees. "Your Cousin Brent and I haven't decided whether we will get married after all. And now I think we'd better go back to the house . . ." She broke off, amazed at the change in Linda's face. She appeared older, suddenly, and the elfin quality which was so charming was utterly gone.

Her face looked pinched and curiously devoid of color.

"It's that Diane Forbes," she burst out suddenly. "She's bad, and I hate her, hate her, hate her!"

Cara, afraid the child would work herself into a tantrum, laid a restraining hand on her shoulders.

"It's wrong to hate people, Linda, especially someone who has done you no harm. When you are older you will understand why Brent and I decided we would be just good friends. It had nothing to do with Diane Forbes, and you must never say that to anyone else. Diane and her father will be here on the Fourth of July, only a few days from now. You must be polite to her while she is a guest in your uncle's home."

"She won't come here. I won't let her." Linda spoke with a chilling finality that was more frightening than her outburst of a few moments before. "She's bad. She can't come here. I hate her! I hate her!"

She twisted herself out of Cara's grasp and ran back to the house without a backward glance.

* * *

Joshua Butler urged them all to go to the country club after dinner. The local tennis tournament was in full swing, he pointed out, and the club would be host to a Westchester group. Usually a special band was imported for an evening such as this, and outside entertainment was arranged.

"We wouldn't want Cara to think we're a dull bunch here at Soundings," Uncle Josh said genially. "Linda and I have our own checkers tournament under way, and we'll play a few games until her bedtime."

"It always amazes me," Paul said, with an amused glance at his uncle, "that you keep up with the doings at the country club in spite of the fact that you actually get there only once a year, on the Fourth of July. Right?"

"I usually attend their Christmas party, too," said Joshua with dignity. "But I'll have you know, young man, I was one of the original founders of that country club before I became sick. We've got to keep up interest and support among the young people, or the place will fold. It costs a fortune these days to maintain a golf course in proper condition. And I marvel the tennis courts are playable at all. We may have to change over to clay courts next year."

"I've heard there isn't the same enthusiasm for tennis that there used to be," Susan commented.

"Interest in it did die out for a while," Paul said, "but now it's coming back. How is your tennis, Cara?"

"Oh, I haven't played in years," Cara said hastily. She did not add she had never played tennis to any extent, any more than she had played golf or gone skiing in the Laurentians or learned to pilot her own plane. She wondered how the group around the dinner table would react if she told them they were a privileged few who could become concerned about playing games when there was so much trouble and sickness in the world. As she caught Uncle Josh's eye, Cara thought she saw a gleam of understanding. It was as if he were saying to her:

"Don't judge us too harshly. I, like you, have seen both sides of the coin. I've known the joy of playing games just for fun, and I've known what it is to be barred from that world forever."

Cara had been to the country club with Brent before. But as they drove up to the sprawling stucco building that night, she was newly aware of how charming the place was. Perhaps, she thought, her brief visit to her own small, stuffy apartment in New York had heightened her awareness of luxurious surroundings.

The special band was a good one, and they were playing an exotic south-of-the-border number. Brent whirled

Cara onto the floor before she could catch her breath.

"One thing I got out of my job in Brazil," he muttered in her ear. "I learned how to do a mean rhumba."

"I'll say," Cara told him, grinning up at him. "You know, I never did quite believe that story about all the hard work you did in the jungles of Brazil or wherever. I shouldn't wonder, if the truth were known, if you went dancing every night with a different *señorita*."

Brent looked at her with narrowed eyes, and finally said, "You could be right. Who am I to deny I am a most charming and attractive fellow? But I want to make one point. As far as I know, none of the *señoritas* is a blonde."

"You're telling me you prefer blondes?"

"I've been trying to tell you that for a long time," Brent said.

It was an evening of fun and laughter. Cara, looking around at the good-looking girls and men, was happy to be part of the group, if only for one evening. But even as she enjoyed it, she wondered if some of the girls, debutantes like Diane Forbes, would not enjoy something more real and purposeful than this butterfly existence where the only object was to have a good time. The thought of Diane Forbes brought back to mind the scene with Linda that afternoon. When she had an opportunity to talk with Susan Evans alone for a moment, Cara thought she'd better mention it.

"I am disturbed at Linda's continuing resentment of Diane Forbes," she told the child's mother. "If it were just a childish resentment, for a childish reason, I wouldn't think it was so dangerous. But, Susan — she has Diane all mixed up with her ideas on voodoo. Frankly, I encouraged her in the White Magic formula she is getting ready to wish on Uncle Josh, but I think she has something in the nature of Black Magic in mind for Diane Forbes."

Linda's mother refused to be

disturbed, Cara realized as Susan talked. She had lived so long in Haiti, with a background of mysticism and exotic rituals, she was unconcerned with its manifestations from a child's point of view. Perhaps, Cara told herself, she was too concerned over what might have been a childish outburst. Right now Linda was probably playing checkers with her Uncle Josh and chortling with glee when she won a game. Cara resolved to put the episode out of her mind.

Later, when she was dancing with Paul, he looked down at her and said:

"You look particularly radiant tonight, Cara. You look, in fact, sort of incandescent, as if you had an electric light inside, lighting you up from within."

"I don't know whether to consider that a flattering remark or not," Cara said. "You make me sound rather as if I were an X-ray picture. I feel as if I were dancing around in my bones, so to speak."

"You know I didn't mean that." Paul was unexpectedly serious. "But I guess I shouldn't be the one to talk like this. I know I haven't got a chance."

Joshua Butler was waiting up for them when they came in shortly after midnight. He sent Bates to ask them to come into his suite before they went upstairs. They found him in excellent spirits, still sitting beside the game table where the checkerboard was set up. The big chair facing the board was empty, and a doll lying on the seat was mute evidence Linda had been there.

Uncle Josh had to hear all about the dance; about how good the orchestra was; about how many people had turned out to welcome the visiting tennis team and the other details of the evening. Cara made Brent show his uncle how proficient he was in the rhumba, and the invalid beamed at them from his wheel chair as they danced across the floor.

Susan Evans, standing beside the empty chair opposite her brother, yawned suddenly and frankly.

"I've had it. If you people want to go on yakking all night, it's all right with me, but I'm going upstairs and get some shut-eye. I suppose I might as well take my daughter's doll upstairs with me." She picked up the small toy and stood looking at it in surprise.

The doll was perhaps eight inches tall and was dressed in yellow organdy with a lace petticoat underneath. But the head of the doll looked strange. The hair was black and matted, and there were daubs of black on the face and dress. If there had been shoes and stockings, they were removed and there was black even on the plastic toes.

"What in the world . . . ?" Susan asked. "I bought Linda this doll last Christmas, and she always liked it particularly. She said it was just the right size."

"Oh, that!" Uncle Joshua said, glancing at the doll indifferently. "Linda brought it with her when she came downstairs, and Fred Bates got her some of my liquid shoe polish when she asked for it."

"Why did she want the shoe polish?" Cara asked fearfully. Her throat felt dry and tight.

"It was a blonde doll," Uncle Josh explained. "Linda said all her dolls were blonde or brown-haired or redheaded, and for some reason she wanted a doll with black hair. Just a childish whim."

Cara stood as if turned to stone. This was no childish whim!

13

CARA did not sleep well that night. She got up several times and walked to her window, which overlooked the rose garden. It looked beautiful and well cared for in the soft light of the moon, and every so often a gentle breeze brought her the intense scent of the Crimson Glory blossoms. She tried to tell herself she was being foolish. No one else was worried about Linda's preoccupation with voodoo, and they knew the child better than she did.

At last, toward morning, Cara fell asleep; contrary to her expectations, she did not dream at all. But it was late when she awoke, and by the time she came downstairs, shamefaced, she knew she was in for a bit of teasing.

"You're a fine gardener," Paul said scornfully, "lying abed while Kelty and

I work our fingers to the bone." He held out a grubby pair of hands.

"Let her alone," Susan said, laughing. "I'll go out and see if I can rustle up a cup of coffee for you, Cara. Then I think you'd better go and talk to my child. She was looking for you. It seems you have some secret project afoot, and she demands a conference. Down by the swimming pool."

Brent wheeled Uncle Josh onto the terrace while Cara was sipping her coffee. Both of them discussed the weather with great animation, as if they were afraid to mention any more personal topic. Paul excused himself to get cleaned up, and Cara thought he winked at his uncle as he passed the wheel chair.

"I don't know why it is," Joshua Butler said, shading his eyes wearily with his hand, "but I am very tired this morning. Not only ordinarily tired, you understand, but completely exhausted. I can't imagine what's the matter with me."

"Maybe your checkers game last night was too much of a strain," Brent said with a grin.

"By the way," Cara asked hesitantly, "did Linda give any reason why she wanted to change the color of her doll's hair?"

"She was carrying it with her when she went down to the swimming pool," Brent told her, "and a pretty miserable-looking, beat-up specimen it is, too. Susan tells me she has over twenty-five dolls; I don't know why she's chosen to carry this one around with her."

"I almost forgot," Uncle Josh said suddenly. "Linda wants you to bring some things you said you would get for her. I asked exactly what she meant, but she wouldn't tell me. She said you would know."

"Yes, I do know," Cara admitted. "I'll have to go to the kitchen and ask Mrs. Kelty for some soy sauce. It's supposed to be pigeon's blood," she explained to Brent. "There's also a demand for green sugar cane, and I trust Mrs. Kelty has green and purple food coloring which I can purloin."

"Is this the special magic formula which is going to make me walk again?" inquired Uncle Josh. "I must say it sounds horrible."

"Well, there's one good thing about it," Cara laughed as she picked up her coffee cup to take it with her to the kitchen. "Linda's recipe calls for a half coconut shell filled with rum, in which all those other ingredients are to be dissolved."

"Ugh!" Uncle Josh's expression, as well as his exclamation, indicated how he felt about Linda'a White Magic. "You know," he added, "I've thought of how I could accept the potion without hurting the child and without putting myself on my death-bed. I had Bates go up to the attic and find a hollow cane I used years ago. I intend to have it right here beside my wheel chair when I am presented with the ungodly stuff."

"Linda is a bright child," Brent

commented. "She will notice if you pour her magic potion into your cane."

"I'm not sure," Cara said, "but I think there must be a sort of chant that goes with drinking this magic potion. At any rate, I'm going to suggest to Linda that she, as the high priestess of the Order of White Magic, close her eyes while she gives the incantation."

"I'm delighted to hear you say so," Uncle Josh said gratefully. "You're a wonderful girl, Cara. And," he added, turning to his nephew, "I said it before and I'll say it again; you're a dope if you don't forget about everyone and really try to make time with this lovely girl."

"You say that," Brent lashed out at him angrily, "and yet you're the one who invited Diane Forbes to come out here again."

"I invited her father," his uncle corrected him. "Anyway, you can tell Paul to run interference for you with Diane."

"When are they coming?" Cara asked.

"Diane phoned about an hour ago," Uncle Josh explained, and suddenly Cara understood why he and Brent had looked so guilty when she came out on the terrace. "She said they'd leave New York right about now; they'll be here for lunch."

"I'm glad you'll have a chance to talk with your old friend," Cara said, and meant it. "As for Diane, she doesn't bother me in the least. Now if you'll excuse me, I'd better pick up those ingredients for Linda and help her complete the formula."

When Cara arrived, carrying the sugar, the soy sauce, the coconut which Mrs. Kelty had bought but which had not yet been opened or dried out, and the other things, Linda was sitting cross-legged on the concrete apron of the pool. She was dressed in a pink sun suit, and she had taken the ribbon off her hair and pulled her hair across her face so that it hung like a brown curtain, swinging back and forth as she swayed from side to side. She was singing an odd, monotonous chant in a language which Cara could not understand.

"Linda, here I am!" Cara called, as she approached the pool. She was determined to ignore Linda's weird actions.

But the child was not to be diverted. She did not respond in any way, but continued her swaying and her chanting as if she were still alone. Then all at once she tossed her head so that her hair flew back and her elfin face was framed by its lank brown strands. Linda opened her eyes and raised something high above her head. In her other hand she held a small silver object which glinted in the sunlight.

Without stopping to think, Cara ran around the pool and snatched the shining object from Linda's hand. It was a small silver letter opener which Cara had noticed on the desk in Uncle Josh's suite. In Linda's other hand was the doll with its hair dyed black. So great was the power of suggestion that for a moment Cara imagined the toy really did resemble Diane Forbes. Linda looked at her with a lowering expression.

"Give me back my silver dagger, my machete."

"Linda, you must stop this nonsense at once. I don't mind helping with your White Magic formula, but now you're doing something very, very naughty."

"I'm going to kill Diane. I hate her!" Linda spoke calmly, as if this statement of fact were all that was necessary.

"You're not going to kill anyone," Cara said grimly, "and you're going to forget this foolishness about hurting people you don't like. Don't you know, Linda," she pleaded, "that Mimbo and some of the other people you knew in Haiti are only victims of superstition? It's a cruel superstition. If we want to hurt another person, and if we have evil thoughts about them, we really hurt only ourselves."

"I can kill her," Linda said, with the finality of a true believer. "Why don't you want her killed? You hate her, too. I know you do."

"I don't hate anybody," Cara said wearily. It seemed to be useless to argue with the child. "But if you don't stop this silliness at once, I am going to take all these ingredients you asked me to get you back to the house and throw them away. I won't help with your magic formula, and I'll see to it your Uncle Joshua doesn't let you go to the country club and watch the fireworks display on the Fourth of July."

The latter threat seemed to be the more effective, Cara noted. Linda gazed for a long time at the bedraggled doll she was holding, apparently weighing in her mind whether or not it was worth-while to carry out her purpose to hurt Diane, if there would be such dire consequences for herself.

"Maybe she won't come," she said at last.

"She is coming. Diane is driving her father out from New York this minute. They will both be here in time for lunch. Both your mother and your Uncle Josh will be terribly hurt if you aren't polite to their guests."

Linda looked up at Cara, and suddenly her mouth twisted in a small, secret smile. Cara did not like the child's expression; somehow it was more disturbing than any expression of anger. But Linda seemed to accept the adult point of view and looked at the doll with almost impersonal distaste.

"Okay."

Linda jumped to her feet, grasping the doll by the legs. Then, before Cara could guess at her intention, she threw the doll with all the force at her command against the far wall of the concrete pool. The plastic toy whacked against the concrete and bounced onto the surface of the pool. There it floated, face down, and Linda turned to Cara with a smile.

"We can forget about Diane now,"

she said cheerfully. "Let's fix up that magic for Uncle Josh."

* * *

The dining room at Soundings was filled with tension. The very air seemed so heavy with hostility it could be cut with a knife, Cara decided. It was a pretty room, not large but gracefully proportioned. The wallpaper was pale green, with a pattern of white leaves, and the woodwork had been painted white. The oval mahogany table, set now with organdy place mats embroidered with daisies, looked inviting and summery.

But Joshua Butler, at the head of the table, was scowling and taciturn. He had waited luncheon for three quarters of an hour, expecting Diane Forbes and her father to arrive at any minute. Just a short time before he had finally refused to wait any longer, and they had all followed him docilely to the table, where he had curtly ordered two of the settings to be removed.

For a while Susan and Paul had made a pretense of normal chatter. Brent had nothing to offer except the suggestion that Diane might have had some obscure problem with the car.

"Then why didn't she hire another car or at least have the courtesy to phone me?" Uncle Josh demanded.

"Perhaps they didn't think it would make any difference if they were a few minutes late," Cara began, and was favored with a contemptuous look from Uncle Josh.

"Diane's father has been here many times before," he snapped. "No — there's no excuse for them being so late. We'll go in and eat, and when they get here I'll certainly give them a piece of my mind."

Paul looked at Cara and shrugged, and Susan settled Linda on a telephone book in her favorite spot to the right of Uncle Josh. The child was dressed in a short-waisted frock of starched yellow pique, with a narrow yellow band holding her shining brown hair back from her face. Cara, looking at her, could scarcely reconcile this perfectly turned out youngster with the fiendish child who had hurled a mutilated doll against the swimming pool wall.

Linda was the only one of the group who apparently was not sensitive to Uncle Josh's angry mood. She chattered to him and to her mother, commenting on the papaya and shrimp salad which was the main course of the luncheon.

"This is just like being back home in Haiti, isn't it, Mommy?" Linda asked with childish delight. "Do you suppose the shrimps swam all the way up here from home just so they could be here when Uncle Josh wanted to eat them?"

Her uncle looked at the child and smiled fondly. Evidently Linda could succeed in dispersing his black mood where the grown-ups had failed.

"I think it more likely the shrimps have nothing to say about it, one way or the other," he told the youngster.

"Wherever they came from, they're delicious," Cara remarked, and both Brent and Paul agreed with her heartily.

"I talked with Mrs. Kelty and suggested a luncheon such as they might serve in Haiti," Susan confessed. "I always liked the food on the plantation, and I thought our guests — " she paused as she realized she had touched on a delicate subject — "would enjoy a slightly different menu," she finished bravely.

Joshua Butler was again glowering at his plate, and Cara finally ventured to voice a thought she had had in mind for some time.

"Is Diane's father in good health?" she inquired. "You know, if he were taken suddenly ill, it might account for the fact that they didn't come. Also, Diane might be too upset to phone."

"Sam Forbes is as healthy as a horse," Joshua Butler grumbled. "I can remember the day when he'd tramp twenty miles or better through

rough country on one of our hunting expeditions in Canada and then sit up most of the night, sitting and telling stories till we finally told him to knock it off."

"I imagine you kept up with him every step of the way," said Paul.

"And topped any of the stories Sam Forbes could tell," Brent added. "But I do agree with you, Uncle Josh: it seems unlikely that Diane's father would become suddenly ill."

"It can happen to anyone," Cara murmured, "especially as he gets older."

Linda had been following the conversation with interest, her bright brown eyes looking first at one and then at the other. Now she fastened her gaze directly on Cara and said with an adult air:

"It isn't Diane's father who's sick."

Paul made some laughing comment about having a clairvoyant in their midst, but Cara scarcely heard him. She felt as if a cold trickle of water was rolling down her spine, and all she could think of was a black-haired doll floating pitifully on the barely rippled water of the swimming pool.

In the distance a telephone sounded, and a few seconds later Fred Bates came to the door. He was white and agitated.

"That was the Meadowbrook Hospital, sir. Mr. Forbes and his daughter have been admitted as patients, and Mr. Forbes insisted you be notified. They were in an accident, I understand."

"An accident!" Joshua Butler looked almost as white as the man-servant.

"That's Diane's driving for you," Paul said sharply. "Are they badly hurt, Bates?"

"I understand Mr. Forbes is okay, sir, except for shock. The hospital said you could call his room — it's 202 — and talk to him on the phone. But Miss Diane is still unconscious, I was told. The car hit the abutment of the bridge, and she was thrown into the water."

14

THEY learned before dinner that night Diane Forbes was going to be all right. She had been thrown into the water with great force, but passing motorists had pulled her out almost at once and, aside from being bruised and pretty well shaken up, she was not injured.

Joshua Butler had discovered these facts in the course of the afternoon. He had talked with his old friend, Sam Forbes, more than once, Cara knew. As he had expected, Josh said with a grin, Sam was proving to be a difficult patient. He was betting Meadowbrook Hospital would have to discharge him the next morning. Otherwise, the hospital routine would be seriously deranged.

Susan Evans had decided she should drive over to see Diane, who was reportedly conscious, but being held under observation. Paul volunteered to go with her, and Cara agreed she would look after Linda. She had promised herself she would have a talk with the youngster anyway, Cara thought grimly. Linda was not going to be allowed to think the silly incantation had been the cause of Diane's accident.

After the others had gone, Cara recommended Josh lie down. She did not like the way he was looking, and to her questions he simply answered he could not shake off his feelings of exhaustion. In his own opinion, Josh Butler told her, he was merely upset because of the bad news they'd had at lunch time.

"Your eyes seem to be troubling you," Cara ventured to comment as Bates started to wheel Joshua to his room. "I've noticed you keep brushing your hand across your eyes."

"Reading too much," Joshua told her shortly. "Sometimes I stare so hard at a page I see double when I look up." At

Cara's expression of alarm, he added sharply, "Now don't you go presuming on the fact that I like you, Cara Merrill. I feel the way I have always felt about doctors and nurses, and I won't have you tricking me into any fancy medical treatment."

Brent looked after his uncle as he retired to his suite, and his expression was much the same as Cara's. He shook his head at her with a rueful smile.

"Stubborn old coot, isn't he?" he observed affectionately. "You're worried, aren't you, Cara?"

"Worried is right," Cara said instantly. "But I haven't given up yet."

"How about driving out to Montauk Point with me, just for the ride?"

"Sorry, Brent, but I have some unfinished business with Linda. Anyhow, I want to be around in case your uncle should need me."

"I never get to see you alone," Brent grumbled. "I'm putting in a bid now for tomorrow night after we have watched the fireworks display with Linda. It's a tradition in these parts," Brent said, grinning, "that after the fireworks you take your best girl out on the golf course — to look at the moon."

Linda was waiting for Cara when she came out on the terrace. The elfin face wore a particularly bland look. Cara lost no time coming to the point.

"You needn't feel so pleased with yourself, Linda," she said, sitting on a chair near the hassock where Linda was perched. Her brief pique skirt was spread out carefully around her.

"I expect I look this way," Linda offered, "because I'm all dressed up. Mommy said I should take off my dress before I take my nap. Are you going to come upstairs with me when I lay down?"

"In a few minutes," Cara said coldly. "But first I want to talk to you. Diane Forbes is going to be all right, you know. She wasn't badly hurt, because she was thrown into the water."

"Just like my doll." Linda nodded, her eyes enormous.

"Stop it!" Cara felt she was not reaching the child. "You must not put your faith in the powers of Black Magic. You could not make an accident happen to Diane Forbes or anyone else."

"She's hurt," Linda said with satisfaction, "and she fell in the water."

"It's just a coincidence," Cara said firmly.

"I don't know what that word means," Linda said, deciding to change the subject. "Can I give Unc' Josh his magic potion this afternoon?"

"You are going to forget all about that potion for Uncle Josh," Cara's tone was firm. "Once and for all you must drop the idea that you can make people sick or well, either by hurting a toy or by making up some weird rum drink."

If there was any efficacy in the formula Linda had concocted, Cara thought grimly, its efficacy in Haiti was more likely due to the liquor than to green sugar cane or anything else. But she was not going to say this to the child.

"Couldn't I give it to him anyway?" Linda asked, looking mutinous. "I've got it all ready."

"I don't want to hear any more about it!" Cara retorted. "And I want you to forget it, too."

"But you said you didn't believe my magic had anything to do with hurting Diane."

"No, it didn't."

"Then why can't I let Unc' Josh have the drink I made up for him? Don't you think it won't work either?"

"Of course it won't work!" Cara spoke before she thought. Suddenly she saw the trap Linda had set for her. If Black Magic was ineffective and had not been responsible for Diane's accident, then White Magic would be ineffective, too. On the other hand, if she forbade Linda to give her uncle the drink, the child might be more convinced than ever that she really had a strange power over health or sickness. Linda brought forth her final argument.

"Unc' Josh expects me to do my White Magic," she reminded Cara. "If you don't let me do it, you'll have to tell him why you won't. Because my Black Magic worked!"

Cara thought for a minute and then said slowly:

"I don't agree with you at all, Linda, but I'm going to compromise with you. For reasons you don't understand, I don't want your Uncle Josh upset by any disagreement between us. So you can give him your magic drink late this afternoon after he has had a chance to rest, just before dinner."

"Thank you," said Linda with dignity.

"All right. We'll go upstairs now, and you can take your nap. Then when you get up I'll take you up to Uncle Josh . . . "

"You can't stay with me," said Linda quickly. "Nobody can be in the room but Unc' Josh and me."

"All right," said Cara impatiently. "I'll arrange it and then leave you alone with him. Now come along upstairs."

She was glad to remember, as she took the child's small hand in hers, that Uncle Josh had prepared for his 'treatment' by being brought a hollow cane.

* * *

As she sat talking with Brent on the terrace, Cara decided she had better make a clean breast of her dealings with Linda. She told him about the scene at the swimming pool in the morning when Linda had attempted to stab her doll with the silver letter opener and then had flung the toy against the far wall of the pool and it had flopped into the water.

As she had expected, Brent was not seriously alarmed. Like Susan, he believed firmly that the child would outgrow her interest in the primitive rituals of voodoo once she went back to school in the fall. However, he agreed with Cara it was best to let her carry through with giving the magic potion to Uncle Josh, since he was already prepared for the experiment and could not be harmed in any way. He promised Cara he would speak to his youthful aunt to caution Linda against any further excursions into magic, either white or black, and with this promise Cara had to be content.

"You know, Carita," Brent said, dismissing the subject, "my Aunt Susan still thinks she has met you somewhere before."

"Would you like me to tell her I was her nurse, briefly, when she was in the hospital?"

"I suppose it doesn't matter now, but it's odd she remembered you so well. I had a point in bringing this up," he added, examining his strong brown hands with care, as if he had never seen them before. "You don't seem to have any idea, Cara, what an effect you have on the people you meet. If I may borrow an idea from my wayward young cousin, you practice a magic of your own."

"My goodness," laughed Cara. "You make me afraid of myself."

"No, I mean it." Brent got to his feet and drew her close to him. Cara knew she should not listen, but for just a few seconds it was sweet to feel his strong arms around her and to know that for the moment he was in earnest.

"No, Brent," she said, drawing away at last. "It won't work. We live in different worlds, you and I. When you asked me to come out here to Soundings as your fiancée, I thought it would be a simple matter to pretend I was someone else."

"You did all right. Uncle Josh has grown very fond of you. He has told me, you see," Brent added with a smile, "if I can get you to say 'yes', he will give us Soundings as a wedding present. My cousin Paul fell in love with you . . . "

"Not really," said Cara. "Paul is in love with love, I think. He can no more resist a flirtation than he can avoid looking like the perennial college boy you told me he was. Paul has a lot of growing up to do."

"Speak of the devil . . . " Brent said, as Paul and Susan drove up to the house.

Diane and her father had had a miraculous escape, they reported as they joined Cara and Brent on the terrace. Sam Forbes, as Joshua Butler had predicted was shouting he would not be held prisoner in the hospital for another hour, and the staff was just about ready to let him go with their blessing. Diane, on the other hand, was beginning to enjoy her place in the spotlight. Because the accident was unusual, and because of the prominence of Sam Forbes as a financier, the scene of the accident had been photographed for television. All of Diane's friends who were in or near New York or on Long Island had immediately gotten in touch with the hospital, and her room was already banked with flowers.

When Susan inquired how her daughter had behaved while she was away, Cara simply said Linda was taking a nap and had been promised she could give the magic potion to her Uncle Josh as soon as she got up.

"I'll go and get my child right now," Susan said, getting up from her chair. "I'm sure my brother has the hollow cane right handy, and we needn't worry about him drinking any of the vile stuff Linda has mixed up. Did you smell it, Cara?"

"It smells to high heaven," Cara agreed. "But if I may make a suggestion, Susan, I think you really should try to discourage Linda from practicing her magic in any way. I agree with Brent she will forget all about voodoo as soon as she goes back to school in the fall. Meantime, she could start her forgetting right now."

"At last I agree with you," Susan declared, smiling warmly at Cara. "I never realized the child had absorbed so much of those odd superstitions which seem to be in the very air down in Haiti. Of course you know voodoo is not practiced openly, and so I blame myself for not seeing that the subject had a special fascination for Linda — simply because it was secret as well as fanciful."

"Oh, let the kid have her fun," Paul said carelessly. "She'll get over it."

"You're talking like a dope," Brent told him. "You bring Linda downstairs, Susan, and I'll go in and see that Uncle Josh is all set for the ceremony."

* * *

It took all of Cara's will power to keep from laughing when Susan brought the child out onto the terrace. Linda might have taken a nap, but it must have been a short one, because some time must have been given to devising the costume she was now wearing.

Linda had taken a pillowcase from

her bed and cut two armholes and a hole for her head from the closed end. The edges were jagged, and the pillowcase had evidently been too long. This Linda had corrected by tying one of her hair ribbons around her waist. With a true instinct for the dramatic, she had chosen a red ribbon and bunched the white pillowcase over it; her ankles and feet were bare.

On her head Linda was wearing a bright red chiffon scarf which Cara remembered Susan sometimes wore. The child had pulled it tight over her hair, crossed the end in the back and tied it in front, under her pointed chin. She had evidently taken advantage of her mother's dressing table as well as her accessories, and had used a lipstick to make a light cross-hatching on each cheek and her forehead.

With both hands Linda was holding the half of a coconut shell. It was almost full of a dark, evil-smelling liquid, and Linda had to walk carefully to keep it from spilling over.

Cara glanced at Paul and was afraid he was going to laugh. She sternly repressed her own impulse and signaled to Susan with a nod that the stage was all set. She and Linda paced slowly down the hall to Uncle Josh's suite. The door was open, and Fred Bates was standing by his master's wheel chair with an anxious expression on his face.

Joshua Butler was not smiling, and Cara wondered if he was playing a role for the benefit of the child or if he actually did not feel well. But she could not ask him; Linda had taken charge.

Placing the coconut shell carefully on the desk against some books so that it would not tip over, Linda firmly insisted Fred Bates and Cara leave the room.

"But couldn't we help you?" Cara asked. She was definitely uneasy about this ritual, now that the moment had come.

"Let Linda do this her own way."

Joshua Butler spoke authoritatively. "Remember this is a magic potion prepared especially for me; I want to give it every chance to work. You and Bates are not to listen at the door, either," Uncle Joshua went on. "Go out to the terrace and wait until you're sent for. Linda will close the door when you go down the hall."

Uncle Josh's tone was fittingly solemn, and there was no doubt Linda was satisfied with her uncle's reactions. But Cara saw the old man's hand rest lightly on the heavy hollow cane standing against his wheel chair. His wink at Fred Bates was so quick she was sure Linda did not see it.

Knowing it was all a bit of play-acting with which Uncle Josh was cooperating for the child's benefit, Cara was amazed at the tension that built up in the small group on the terrace. They were all silent, listening, although there was nothing to hear, for some half-expected, half-feared sound from Uncle Joshua's wing. Cara was reminded of her first glimpse of Soundings, and of how she had thought the sprawling brown house seemed brooding — even sinister.

During the weeks she had been a guest there, the house and the people in it had become so familiar she had lost the sense of menace which she had felt at first. Now it returned stronger than ever, and involuntarily she shivered.

Paul was smoking one cigarette after another, his gestures quick and nervous. Brent paced up and down the terrace, looking out toward the Sound. Susan Evans sat in one of the wicker chairs, but she was leaning forward, with her hands tightly clasped in her lap. Fred Bates stood near the door as if ready to dash inside. Cara thought she herself was being calm and cool; she was startled to find the handkerchief she was holding suddenly came apart in her hands.

Then it happened.

There came an unearthly scream — a scream that seemed to come from no human throat. The sound was high and wailing, and it held the fear of all men when confronted by the forces of the unknown. It stopped abruptly and then came again, even shriller and more piercing.

"That's Linda!" Susan Evans was on her feet, but the others stood still, as if rooted to the spot. The white-clad figure of Linda burst out of the door, looking like the very embodiment of the wild shriek that had preceded her.

"Mommy! Mommy! Unc' Josh is dead!"

15

CARA never knew how she got from the terrace into Uncle Josh's suite, after Linda had flung herself into her mother's arms. Thinking about it afterward, she supposed her long training had taken over and she had moved instinctively.

Uncle Josh was still in his wheel chair, slumped over to one side, one arm dangling so it almost reached the floor. He seemed to be scarcely breathing, and Cara's hand flew to unfasten his shirt and tie. Fred Bates reached over and straightened his master gently.

"We must get him into bed," Cara said, and Paul and Brent instantly leaped to the wheel chair. Cara stood aside as they lifted Joshua Butler's unconscious form. Bates was standing at the door to the bedroom, and Cara followed. It all happened in a matter of seconds.

Cara moved over to the bed. She did not have time to be surprised to find it was a hospital bed. Bates had already raised the head, and she saw there was a tank of oxygen standing on the floor. He held out the mask to her.

"Would you adjust this, please?" Bates said. Even as Cara's fingers automatically fitted the mask over the unconscious man's face, she was thinking this was an emergency for which Joshua Butler had long prepared. Then he must have known he had a heart condition!

"I'll call the hospital at Glen Rock," Brent said, standing beside the bed. "Do you think I should ask them to send an ambulance?"

"No," said Cara. "Since we have the oxygen, your uncle is all right here at home for the moment. But ask them to send a doctor right away. Unless there is a doctor nearer at hand?" Cara said, with a questioning look at Bates. "One of his own choice?"

"Mr. Butler wouldn't have a doctor, miss," Bates said; "in the last few years, anyway."

"I think the hospital at Glen Rock will send someone," Brent said, going toward the phone. "They seem to know Uncle Josh, as I found out while Linda was there."

It was Dr. Crane who came in a short time. He approved of what Cara and Bates had done to relieve Joshua's distress, and he gave him medication. Cara told him she was a nurse, and he agreed it would be better not to move Joshua to a hospital, since he could be taken care of at home. But he did urge Brent to call a heart specialist immediately and have him come to Soundings at once.

"My uncle's pretty rabid on the subject of doctors," Paul said to Dr. Crane, who looked impatient.

"He has no choice now," the young doctor said. "Anyway, judging from the fact that your uncle has a hospital bed

NM16

and keeps a tank of oxygen and a mask near at hand, I should say Mr. Butler had already been apprised of his condition, and his well-publicized attitude toward the medical profession was mainly a pose. Anyhow, he must see a specialist at once."

When the doctor had gone, Cara left Bates and went to her room. As quickly as possible she took off the chiffon dinner dress she had been wearing and put on her starched uniform. There was, she knew, a certain psychological value, both to the patient and to the household, in having a uniformed nurse in attendance.

When she entered Joshua Butler's bedroom a short time later, Bates got up from his chair beside the bed. He did not seem surprised to see her in white with her cap pinned on her hair.

"You knew?" Cara whispered.

"Yes, miss," the man whispered back, and there was just the ghost of a smile on his lips. "I've been with Mr. Butler for five years now, and he has always treated me as a friend. I was the only one who knew he kept the oxygen tank handy and that his raving against doctors and medicine was only a pose. I'm glad you're here, Miss Merrill," Bates said as he slipped away.

Joshua Butler continued to sleep. He was breathing easily and his pulse was almost normal, Cara noted. She herself began to breathe easily for the first time in more than an hour.

"I've brought you a tray," Brent whispered, a short time later, from the door. "It's on the desk."

"Thank you," said Cara. "Your uncle will be all right when he wakes up, I think."

"I have a heart specialist coming out from New York," Brent told her. "He should be here in about an hour."

Still later it was Susan who looked into the bedroom. Cara went into Uncle Josh's study to talk with her for a minute.

"How is Linda?" she asked Susan.

"I hope she doesn't blame herself for what happened. I'm sure her uncle didn't get a chance to drink any of her magic potion. I found it spilled on the rug, and the coconut shell had rolled under the chair. Of course he was going to pour it into the hollow cane anyway, but the attack came on too suddenly."

"I've told Linda she was not responsible," Susan said. "But as you can imagine, the child was frightened out of her wits. And there is no doubt about it — she will never try to practice White Magic again. Did Brent tell you the heart specialist is on his way?"

"Yes, he told me when he brought me a dinner tray," Cara said. "There's nothing more we can do for your brother now until the doctor gets here. But I'll stay right beside him."

Susan Evans smiled at her and said slowly, as her eyes traveled over the white uniform and fastened at last on the nurse's cap with its narrow black band:

"Of course. Now I know where I saw you before, Cara Merrill. You were working in the hospital where I had my operation; you came in one day when my special duty nurse was called away. You're a wonderful nurse, Cara, and I'm delighted to know my brother is going to be in your care."

The next day Joshua Butler was resting comfortably. The heart specialist had been a man of few words with a manner as curt as Uncle Joshua's. He did not give anyone in the household a chance to voice an opinion. He simply stated Mr. Butler could remain at home if he were kept completely quiet; that he was glad to see a registered nurse in attendance and that his instructions were to be followed to the letter. The specialist declared he would not return on the holiday unless some unforseen complication occurred, when he could be reached by phone. He gave Cara a private number. He would call again at eleven o'clock on the morning of the fifth.

"Sort of inspires confidence, doesn't he?" Paul asked, grinning. "Even if Uncle Josh had been in his usual form, I doubt if he could have made our man give an inch."

"He's a very fine physician," Cara told Paul. "His reputation is national. I must get back to your uncle, Paul; I only came out on the terrace for a breath of air."

"Ah, yes, Nurse Merrill," Paul retorted, looking at her uniform meaningly. "You know I'm still having a hard time trying to adjust myself to you as a nurse. How come anyone as beautiful as you elected to spend her time with sick people?"

"The answer is very simple." Cara smiled back at him. "I like people, whether they are sick or well. And as for being beautiful, for which compliment I thank you, sir, all nurses are beautiful to the person who needs their care."

"How about tonight?" Paul demanded. "You know, the fireworks . . . "

"I hadn't thought about it. Better

ask Brent." Cara hurried back to her patient.

During the afternoon Uncle Josh was so much better that he managed to take the liquids which had been ordered for him and even tried to belittle the seriousness of his attack. Cara discovered that Brent and Susan between them had been busy figuring out a careful schedule so she could accompany Susan, Paul and Brent when they took Linda to see the fireworks.

Her protests were met with the incontrovertible fact: Uncle Josh needed little care at the moment, but only complete rest. Fred Bates, who spelled her when she had lunch and again at dinner time, was ready to spend at least two hours more sitting beside the bed while Cara was at the country club.

"We've already told Uncle Josh about this arrangement, and it has his full blessing," Brent said, looking at her with a special intentness. "If you don't go to see the fireworks but insist upon sitting in his room, Uncle Josh may be afraid you think he's likely to have a relapse."

"You shouldn't have said anything about it," Cara said reprovingly.

Brent held up his hands to halt her scolding. "It wasn't my fault. Uncle Josh asked to see Linda while you were at lunch, and he was insistent she see the fireworks tonight. Then he went ahead and planned the rest of the party; he got Fred Bates to tell us we were all to go. Of course, I'll bring you home before eleven."

As they drove up to the country club a little after eight o'clock, Cara was glad that she had agreed to come. She had been under quite a nervous strain, she realized now, for the last twenty-four hours. Now the worst was over. Linda, squeezing into the front seat between Cara and Brent, was full of childish anticipation over the fireworks she was going to see. She and Brent were talking a lot of nonsense about riding some of the rockets up to the moon, and Linda could scarcely answer for giggling.

Cara had left Joshua Butler lying back against his pillow, looking almost like his old self. He could still run his household and tell people what to do, even though he was confined to his bed, his sly smiled seemed to say. She was free to relax and enjoy the evening.

Several members of the club, men who appeared to be about Uncle Josh's age, inquired solicitously about Josh and gave Brent messages to take back to him. Linda joined a group of about fifteen youngsters who were being amused by a clown who was pretending to be frightened by the tiny firecrackers he was exploding. They were among the last arrivals, Cara saw when they went out on the terrace where chairs had been set up for the adults to watch the display. The children were clustered in the paved courtyard below, with watchful attendants to see they did not get too near the scene of operations.

"You look almost as thrilled as Linda," Susan whispered to Cara with a little chuckle. "I think you're going to enjoy the display. They really do a nice job here."

"Does it take long?" Cara asked.

"Only half an hour. But don't worry about my brother. Brent and I have talked it over, and he will get you back to the house in good time."

"I'll leave as soon as the show is over," Cara declared. "Oh, what a wonderful set piece! It looks like a fiery fountain." She did not see the smile Susan gave Brent behind her back.

Half an hour later, when the last set had blazed and died against the night sky, Cara stood up with a sigh. She shook herself as if coming back from a land of enchantment. Brent put his hand under her elbow and guided her through the crowd.

"Susan and Paul are up ahead," she pointed out, "over there to the left.

Oh, I suppose they're going to pick up Linda."

"That's right," Brent said, urging her still further in the opposite direction. "They're going to pick up Linda and take her home."

"Then we'd better hurry, or they'll leave without us."

"That's the general idea," said Brent. "I've arranged with the manager of the club to have them taken back in one of the club's cars. They'll leave the convertible for us."

"Oh," said Cara. She did not know whether or not she was pleased with this high-handed treatment, as if she were a person with no sense of responsibility. After a moment Brent added:

"If you don't want to hear what I have to say, Cara, we'll leave right now. But I think you do owe me a chance to plead my case."

"You did mention the golf course, didn't you?" Cara murmured. "I must say it looks like a popular spot." Glancing over her shoulder, she saw the green was dotted with strolling couples.

Brent knew his way around. They walked toward the grove at the edge of the green and, turning suddenly came upon a small bench. Cara sank onto it gratefully, her knees trembling. She knew Brent was going to ask her to marry him, and she knew she would have to refuse. Hoping to forestall his question, she said in a troubled tone:

"Before you say anything, Brent, let me remind you of something I said in New York, when you came to get me. We do live in different worlds, you know."

"I'd be pleased to know what you think my world is," Brent said gravely.

"The world of Long Island estates and country clubs and debutantes who make news whether they are in this country or abroad. It's a world to which you were born, and where you belong."

"And what is your world?" Brent asked, as if he were seeking information.

"My world is one of service and dedication. It's a singularly rewarding world, Brent, although if you're not part of it, the rewards may seem intangible. But believe me, they are very real."

Brent sat down beside her suddenly, and Cara wished he had not. When he was so close, with his hands on her arm and his cheek against her hair, it was hard to think straight. It was hard to think at all.

"All right, Carita. You've had your say; now I'll have mine. You have a very nice argument there; the only trouble is it's all wrong."

"But . . . "

Brent kissed her lightly to silence her. "But me no buts, my darling. My world is far removed from grand estates and country clubs. I have lived most of my working life in rough construction camps on the edges of dusty deserts and in the middle of steaming jungles. Much of the time I've worried about supplies that don't get delivered and members of my crew who come down sick with malaria or something else. I never have enough time to finish a job, it seems to me, before a rainy season sets in or a tornado strikes or even an earthquake. I was once caught in a mild earthquake."

"I never dreamed it was like that with you," Cara said wonderingly. "Your work is concerned with emergencies, isn't it? In a way, it's like a nurse's work in a hospital. You never know when the unexpected may happen." She turned and looked at him, but he was gazing above her head, his eyes narrowed on a distant point.

"I want to be fair," he said at last. "The life I am offering you is not one of luxury and ease. It's a tough and dangerous existence, make no mistake about it. And I have no right to ask you to share it — unless you love me. You could have a glamorous life somewhere here or abroad, I know," he said humbly. "You are so lovely, you could have anything you wanted."

"But suppose I don't want a life of

luxury and ease," Cara said demurely. "What am I offered instead?"

"All the love I can give you," Brent said huskily, "forever and wherever we are. Oh, Cara, I need you so!"

"Why didn't you tell me that before?" Cara murmured, her lips against his cheek. "That's what I've been waiting to hear."

"You mean . . . ?"

"I mean I love you, Brent, but I didn't believe I had any place in your life. Now that I know, I can tell you I love you, darling. I didn't dare admit it, even to myself. But now I can say it: I love you, Brent, love you, love you . . . "

Other titles in the Linford Romance Library:

A YOUNG MAN'S FANCY
Nancy Bell

Six people get together for reasons of their own, and the result is one of misunderstanding, suspicion and mounting tension.

THE WISDOM OF LOVE
Janey Blair

Barbie meets Louis and receives flattering proposals, but her reawakened affection for Jonah develops into an overwhelming passion.

MIRAGE IN THE MOONLIGHT
Mandy Brown

En route to an island to be secretary to a multi-millionaire, Heather's stubborn loyalty to her former flatmate plunges her into a grim hazard.